Take Me, Cowboy

Take Me, Cowboy

A Copper Mountain Rodeo Novella

Jane Porter

TULE
PUBLISHING

Tule Publishing First Printing, July 2017

The Tule Publishing Group, LLC

ISBN 978-1-947636-00-2

Dedication

For my Girls—Megan, Lilian and CJ. You are the best.

For Rebecca—Thank you for joining the madness.

And for my Guy—'Cause you are still so smokin' hot.

Chapter One

"I CAN'T DO it, Jenny. I can't go through with this."

The warm dry autumn wind whipped Jenny Wright's wedding veil up above her shoulders, fine lace grazing her cheek. Having lived the past ten years in Chicago, Jenny had forgotten the wind that whistled from Yellowstone, down through Paradise Valley, turning the ranching valley into a wind tunnel.

The wind snapped and crackled now, the gusts as much a part of Marietta as the iconic peak of Copper Mountain jutting behind the small, sleepy Montana town. Marietta had surged to life in the late eighteen-hundreds before nearly dying, when the copper boom proved to be nothing more than a hiccup and all the investors and prospectors packed up and moved away.

It'd been a hundred and twenty-some years since then, but it was still hard to make a living in Marietta.

It's why she'd left town as soon as she'd graduated from high school. It's why she'd been determined to never move back.

She'd only come home for her wedding. Only come

home to make her family proud.

Jenny gently plucked the delicate veil from her small diamond and pearl earring before it tore. "I didn't catch that, honey," she said, smashing the sudden rush of adrenaline flooding her veins.

No need to panic, she told herself. It was so windy today, and others might not like the gusts, but the wind had blown all the clouds north, leaving the sky above Marietta a perfect brilliant blue, and the wind had made it hard to hear.

Because for a moment there, it sounded as if Charles said he wouldn't marry her. But that didn't make sense. He and his family were here. The guests were here. The minister was here, all in the church waiting.

Waiting.

Her stomach rose and fell. She swallowed hard, fighting a sudden rush of nausea. She hadn't slept well last night, nervous. Excited.

Excited, she silently insisted. Not terrified. Or sad. She would never be sad. This was the right decision. This was the best decision. It was.

It had to be.

"Can you say that again?" she asked him, fighting both her veil and the horrible rush of adrenaline.

He hesitated.

She stared at his mouth, focusing on his lips, not wanting to miss a thing this time.

And looking at his mouth, she tried to feel reassured. Because she knew him. She'd worked for his company for years, first as an administrative assistant in Human Resources, then as a manager, before he'd hand picked her to be his assistant, and then his girlfriend. His woman. It hadn't happened overnight. At least the love part.

The love part had been tricky, but she loved him now. He'd been in her life a long time, and he'd been good to her. Better than any man had been to her.

And just like that her chest squeezed and her eyes burned and her throat threatened to close.

Maybe it wasn't the wild fierce passionate love you read about in books, but it was steady and kind, and based on respect. Mutual respect.

They were good for each other.

"Charles?" she whispered, fighting the awful aching lump in her throat.

He just stared at her, gray eyes shadowed. "Things got out of hand, Jenny. I'm sorry."

"I don't understand."

He said nothing.

She bit down so hard into her bottom lip she tasted lipstick and blood.

Keep it together, she told herself. Keep it together. You can fix this. You can. You've fixed everything else in his life… you can fix this, too.

She masked her panic with one of her professional smiles. Thank God for a stressful career. The workload and deadlines had taught her to cope with pressure. She'd learned how to be strong. "I hear almost every bride and groom experience some cold feet. It's natural." She managed a lopsided smile. "We wouldn't be normal if we didn't have a few pre-wedding jitters."

"Jenny, I'm not going to marry you."

She suddenly pictured her family—Mama, Daddy, Grandma, her sisters and the rest of her bridesmaids—dressed in their new, expensive, and uncomfortable fancy clothes. This was a big day for the Wrights and they hadn't wanted to disappoint. Scrubbed clean, perfumed, shoes shining, waiting in the church, fighting nerves of their own.

"I'm shocked," she said calmly, her voice firm, composed. My God, she was good at hiding pain. Hiding her own feelings. Her needs.

But then, she didn't assert her needs anymore.

Being Charles Monmouth's assistant had taught her oh so very well.

"I should have said something last night," he said, looking over her head to avoid meeting her gaze.

She squeezed her bouquet to keep from making a sound. He knew last night? He'd been thinking about this ever since then?

"When did you know?" she whispered.

"During the rehearsal. In the church." He reached up to rub his forehead, then sighed. "Earlier, actually." He sighed again, before grimacing. "Okay. For quite some time....

Actually."

Actually.

Actually.

She almost laughed out loud. It was that, or cry. And she wasn't going to cry. This was her wedding day.

"I've had second thoughts for awhile," he added. "I'm sorry."

And yet they'd made love last night. She'd pleasured him before dinner and then they'd had sex after.

He didn't seem to have a problem with the sex part.

Just the marrying part.

But no, she couldn't go there. It was unkind. She wouldn't be unkind. Charles wasn't being unkind.

He was afraid. Nervous. Normal emotions.

"Why didn't you talk to me last night?" She plucked the veil back again, hating the delicate lace now. And the wind.

And the fear clawing at her that he was going to walk, and she'd be left here, with nothing.

Just debt. And shame. And heartbreak.

The heartbreak would be for her mother who was so proud of Jenny. This day meant so much to Mama, who'd never had a church wedding with bridesmaids and flower girls and—

Stop. Stop right there, she told herself, blinking hard. Everything would work out. She just had to stay calm, just had to focus. *Think. Figure out what's wrong.*

But she couldn't think clearly, not when she knew that

the bridal party would be fidgeting at the back of the church and one hundred and fifty people were whispering in the pews, wondering about the delay.

"Charles, what's happening? Talk to me."

"There's not much to say." He glanced at her, and then swiftly away, his expression as stiff, hard, nearly as hard as his voice. "I just realized this won't work. Not long term. Better we face it now than suffer the consequences later."

"Why wouldn't it work?"

"We're too different. We come from completely different backgrounds."

"You've known for years… ever since you made me your personal assistant."

"But it didn't… bother… me… before."

She had a sudden sick feeling that she knew where this was going and she didn't like it. Not one bit. "Why does it bother you now?"

His shoulder rolled. A shrug.

She wouldn't let him off that easy. "Charles, explain. Please."

For a moment she didn't think he was going to answer and then he exhaled hard. "Are you marrying me for my money?" His jaw tightened. He looked away. "Are you a gold digger?"

Her mouth opened, closed, just like a trout gasping for air out of water. A gold digger? "That's a terrible thing to say."

He wouldn't look her in the eye. He shrugged instead.

She stared at his tuxedo-clad shoulder, anger and pain churning inside her, making her sick.

His words wounded, but it was his careless, indifferent shrug that cut most.

How dare he shrug now? Shrug. A shrug.

A thirty-seven year old man shrugging instead of speaking. Shrugging to hide. Shrugging because he wasn't a man at all.

Tears burned her eyes and her throat ached and she wanted to take her flowers and slap Charles Monmouth III. Slap sense into him. Slap him to make him feel again and speak to her kindly again and remind him that just last night he'd whispered he needed her and wanted her and…

She swallowed hard, brows tugging as she tried to remember what else he'd said last night as they'd been in bed.

Had he said anything about love? Had he said anything about wanting to marry her… or had it just been sex last night? Lust?

She lifted her chin, lips trembling before she pressed them together, into a thin line.

Had he ever loved her?

Or had it always been lust…?

"I'm not a gold digger," she added fiercely, so close to throwing her flowers. If not at him, then across the sidewalk, into the street.

This was awful. Worse than awful. And soon everyone

would know.

Everyone would know that Charles Monmouth of Lake Forest, Illinois wasn't going to marry Jenny Wright of Marietta, for no other reason than she wasn't good enough.

She didn't come from a fancy town or an affluent enclave where all the big houses were. No, she was from the north side of town. The Northside of Marietta. On the north side of the train tracks.

"You're killing me," she whispered, picturing her mom and dad and sisters in the church. Her friends Chelsea and Sage. She could see them all and knew that soon—just minutes from now—the joy would be dashed, replaced by disappointment, and pain.

"I'm not sure how this will work… later. Back in Chicago," Charles said stiffly, rubbing at the back of his neck now.

He was probably getting one of his tension headaches. He got them so frequently. She'd become an expert masseuse, working away at his neck and shoulders, easing those knots, helping him relax.

Her mother had warned her years ago to be careful.

Her mother had warned her that powerful men, rich men, had their own rules.

Jenny had laughed away her mother's concerns. *I'm not a little girl anymore, Mama. I know what I'm doing. And he's not using me. He loves me. He's going to marry me.*

She choked back a nearly hysterical laugh.

No, he's not.

Jenny reached up to quickly wipe the dampness from the corners of her eyes before the tears could smudge her makeup. "Did you ever love me?" she asked.

"Jenny."

He sounded exasperated.

She arched a brow. "Yes?"

"It's not an issue of love."

"It's not?"

"No."

"Then what is it, Charles?"

"It's… our differences. Our backgrounds. We come from very different cultures."

"We're both white, Anglo-Saxon, and Protestant."

He tugged on his tie. "You know what I mean."

Unfortunately, she did.

He was rich and she was poor. That was different enough. He didn't need to say another word. She knew this part. Knew how it would go.

Suddenly she hated her Vera Wang bridal gown. It was a gown her parents couldn't afford, and so she'd bought it herself, using nearly all of her savings because she'd wanted to be special today. Wanted to feel like a princess. The princess in a fairy tale.

Stupid. She was so stupid.

"So it's over," she said quietly, grateful her voice didn't crack, and her eyes were almost dry.

He took a breath, shook his head. "I'm sorry."

She looked at him from beneath her lashes, sorry, too, but for completely different reasons. She was sorry she'd exposed her family to his scorn. Sorry she'd asked him here, to her world, and her home. Sorry she'd allowed herself to be swayed by his influence. His money. Because she'd be lying if she hadn't been teased by the possibility of security. Of stability. Of having a home that wouldn't be taken from her… a place where she could raise her own family, knowing her children would never have to struggle, or go hungry, or start the first day of school without new school supplies.

"Jenny, I just wish you'd told me," Charles said now, his tone almost agonized, revealing more emotion than he had since last night, making love to her. "Told me about your father, and everything. It would have been better… before."

Her chin lifted again. "But I did."

"You said your father worked at a hospital."

"And he does."

"He's the *janitor.*" Charles shoulders shifted inside the elegant tux jacket. "And that's fine, but he's… struggled… to keep his job. He struggled to keep any job."

"He's had struggles, yes, but he's a good man."

"He's an alcoholic."

"In recovery." Her face burned. "He's been sober for years."

"Two years. If that."

"He made a mistake, and he went back to AA, but he was sober for almost five years before he'd… had the drink."

"*Drinks.*" Charles gave her a peculiar look. "Alcoholism runs in families. It's a genetic thing."

She said nothing.

He pushed on. "My father ran a credit check on your family. Wasn't a glowing report. Wasn't even remotely glowing. Or good."

She felt sick all the way through her. Her head hurt. Her heart hurt. Her bones hurt. "We've had struggles, but that has nothing to do with me. Or with us—"

"But it does. If we have children, they have that DNA... the genetics. I didn't fully realize, until here, that I should have listened to my gut. My instincts. You're a lovely girl, Jenny. Beautiful and sweet and kind and good—"

"Please. Stop. I've heard enough. I've had enough. I'm not a dog."

"I'll give you excellent references—"

"Not necessary," she choked, voice strangled, heart lurching, sick. Appalled.

She wasn't just a discarded bride, but an... out of work employee?

It was all she could do to keep from throwing her bouquet at his head. She was a good shot, too. She could level him with one hard, furious throw.

"Well, if you change your mind," he said, sounding troubled... concerned.

Jenny laughed. She couldn't help it. "I would never ask you for a referral," she said, laughing again. Laughter was good. It kept her from crying. "You'd be the last person I would go to for help."

"What? Why?"

"You're an ass!" She laughed, shook her head, disgusted. But not just with him. She was disgusted with herself. She knew with a flash of blinding insight that this was all her fault.

She'd allowed herself to be dazzled by his family fortune. Charles descended from the titans of industry, those turn-of-the-century Monmouths who'd once been the governor of Illinois and ruled Chicago as scions of society.

She knew now that she'd fallen in love with his beautiful, extravagant world as much as she had fallen in love with him.

She knew, too, that her parents would be shattered. They'd been so pleased their oldest daughter had found her perfect man.

And landing Charles Victor Monmouth III had been a fairy tale come true. That is, until now.

But the fairy tale was over. And she knew exactly what was about to happen.

Charles Victor Monmouth III was going to walk away, and leave her alone in the parking lot in her stunning Vera Wang.

Jenny couldn't have it, wouldn't have it.

He could dump her, reject her, but he would not walk away from her now. She would do the walking. She would turn her back on him. She was finished with stupid dreams and fairy tales.

She was not Cinderella, and he was no prince. She was just a girl from the wrong side of the tracks and she'd grown up taking some hard hits. This was certainly another brutal blow, but it would not break her. Charles would not break her.

Jenny Wright had come too far to be broken now.

With a regal sweep of her arm, she scooped up the train of her shimmering bridal gown, letting it fall in a pool of gleaming white silk across her wrist. Head high, shoulders back, she turned away from Charles and walked from the parking lot to the sidewalk, and just kept walking.

She didn't know where she was going.

But it didn't matter.

Obviously, she'd need to return to the church and deal with her family and the one hundred and fifty guests waiting inside, but for now, they could wait. Everyone and everything could wait. She needed a minute to herself.

A minute to gather herself. Salvage her pride.

It was going to be okay.

It would have to be okay.

That was her job now.

Chapter Two

COLTON THORPE HADN'T been back to Marietta in two years and he drove slowly through the historic downtown, noting new businesses that had opened, and local favorites still operating like the Palace Movie Theatre, Grey's Saloon, and Main Street Diner, which is where he promised his mother he'd take her tonight.

His mom loved the old diner. It was one of the places she was still comfortable going in her wheelchair, but then her mother had been the head cook at the diner for twenty years, from the nineteen-forties to the sixties and she liked going to the diner whenever he came to town. Which wasn't often.

He hadn't meant to stay away so long, but with his marriage ending and his demanding travel schedule, it was hard getting home.

Not that Marietta felt like home anymore.

This is where other people lived—his mom, his sister, a few high school friends. He lived in Tulsa now.

Not that that felt like home, either. Tulsa was his ex-wife Lisa's home. Quite honestly, he didn't know where he belonged anymore. Maybe that's why he was most comfortable on the road, sleeping in motels, hotels, and the cab of his truck when too tired or sore to drive another mile. He had a house in Tulsa but it was mostly empty. He was mostly empty, which made it easy to get lost in his dangerous, adrenaline-fueled career of sawdust floors, bright lights, and noisy, crowded arenas. He was okay with the sweat, blood, and pain. Bull-riding was just another metaphor for life. What didn't kill you, made you stronger.

Colton turned the corner, passing Crawford Park with its handsome gray stone county court house and snow-capped Copper Mountain soaring behind.

Big trees bordered the city park, the leaves just starting to change, and the breeze rustled the green, rust and gold leaves, catching some, sending others scuttling down the road.

He braked at Church Avenue, watching the swirling leaves, then glanced right, left, and was just about to continue east when a flash of white caught his eye.

Gaze narrowing, he leaned on his steering wheel to get a better look.

A girl in blinding white, standing on the corner.

He'd intended to continue to Bramble Lane but impulsively he turned left, onto Church, driving toward the girl on the street corner, her gown reflecting light, dazzling white light, with bits of iridescent sparkle and shimmer.

He eased off the accelerator as he approached her, intrigued.

Princess at the bus stop.

Cinderella without a glass coach.

As he drew near, her head turned. She looked at him. Her veil had been pushed back from her face. Her eyes were brown. A brilliant liquid brown.

She'd been crying. Or maybe trying not to cry.

His chest tightened, the sensation sharp, and hard, and unexpected.

Then her gaze lifted another inch, and she looked unflinchingly into his eyes. Her gaze held his, challengingly. She dared him to speak. Dared him to criticize.

Princess bride.

Air hitched in his chest, his fingers tightened on the hard steering wheel. Princess Bride, like the movie by the same name. He'd loved that film as a kid.

And here was a girl who looked just like the princess in the movie.

This girl on the street corner was that beautiful.

Film star beautiful, with gold hair. Lots of it. And cheekbones like a question mark, high and full, never mind the sweet, soulful mouth that tilted down at the corners even as tears darkened the thick black fringe of eyelash.

Beauty broken from the Beast, looking for a way home.

Colton, who'd learned long ago not to get involved in other people's business, told himself not to get involved now. But he couldn't just leave her here. Couldn't ignore her. Princess brides didn't belong on street corners.

He rolled down his truck window. "You okay, darlin'?"

She glanced at him, then away, and nodded, her gaze riveted on the majestic peak of Copper Mountain behind them. "Yes."

Her voice was soft, low, and it made his chest ache again. He didn't understand the pang, just knew that something wasn't right and he couldn't continue to Bramble Lane and admire Marietta's big old houses when Beauty stood here all alone. "Need a ride somewhere?"

She shook her head once, briefly. "No. But thank you."

She was dismissing him. He understood, and didn't blame her. She was a princess and he was a dirty, dusty unshaven cowboy driving a dirty, dusty old truck. "Waiting for the bus?"

She shook her head again.

"Good," he said. "'Cause I don't think there is bus service this late on Saturday afternoon. At least, the last bus used to stop around three and it's got to be going on four."

"Probably closer to four-thirty," she agreed. The wind caught at her veil, blowing it up, haloing her head. She reached up to catch it, and tugged it back down. "It's breezy."

"Almost always is. You're not from around here."

"No, I am. I was born here, but I haven't lived here in years. I just came home for my—" she broke off, looked away, two spots of color high in her cheeks. For a moment the only sound was the wind rustling leaves, and the cling-clang as an empty aluminum can bounced across the St. James parking lot.

But she didn't need to finish her sentence. Wasn't necessary to complete it. She'd come home for her wedding and yet here she was, alone on Church and First Street, as if all brides hung out on street corners on their wedding day. "You look beautiful."

She made a soft, hoarse sound and her eyes welled with tears. She bit hard into her lower lip. "It's the dress." She lightly ran her fingertips across her middle, skimming the silk. "It cost a fortune."

And then she looked up, into his eyes, and he hitched a breath, feeling as though he'd been punched in the gut. There was so much in her eyes, so much emotion. He could see her hurt. Feel her pain.

He didn't like it.

He didn't know her. He didn't want to feel this, or anything, not for her. Not for any woman. He'd provide for his mom and sister, but he was done with emotional entanglements. Women felt good and smelled good and were good for some old fashioned loving, but he didn't need problems. And this princess was most definitely a problem.

"Wedding dresses usually do," he said.

A flash of fire lit her eyes. Pride squelching the hurt, making her look more like a warrior than a princess in distress. "You know a lot about wedding gowns, cowboy?"

He didn't know if it was the words or her tone that made

him smile, but he did. Reluctantly. He liked her fire a hell of a lot more than the sadness. Pride was good. Backbone even better. "I've seen Say Yes to the Dress before."

She shook her head, disgusted.

"Not by choice," he added.

"Of course not," she said, her chin notching up.

"So when is the wedding?" he asked.

"Now. At least, it was supposed to be now. Everyone's there, waiting."

Thus all the cars in the St. James parking lot, and the overflow cars lining the street. "And you're what… running away?"

"No." She exhaled hard. "My groom did."

"Cold feet?"

She smiled, a tough not-going-to-cry smile which made his chest burn as if he'd swallowed whiskey straight. "Cold heart." Her lips twisted ruefully. "Turns out I'm not good enough for him."

Colton's gaze swept her, from the top of her head to the toes of her elegant white silk shoes. "How's that possible? You look like a fairy tale princess come to life."

Her eyes locked with his and for a moment she looked open and soft and so very, very sweet. And then her slim shoulders twisted and she lifted her chin again. "Ah, cowboy, but that's the problem. Fairy tales don't exist."

And then she flashed him another tough-girl smile that would have broken his heart if he'd still had one, before scooping up the train of her dress and walking away from him, heading for the entrance to the gray gothic-inspired St. James, the stunning Protestant church he'd never been in, because this wasn't his side of town. He'd been raised in north Marietta, where rent was cheap and opportunity non-existent. That's why he'd left Marietta the day after his high school graduation. He left the very first chance he could.

~

JENNY WALKED QUICKLY away from the cowboy in the truck, surprised. Unnerved. Goose bumps covering her arms, her skin prickling all the way down her back.

Colton Thorpe.

Colton Thorpe was back in town.

She clutched her fragrant bouquet, her steps unsteady as she climbed the stairs to the church.

Colton. Wow.

Wow.

Talk about a blast from the past.

She'd had the most ridiculous thing for him. One of those hopeless crushes that kept her awake at night and filled a diary with adolescent longing…

The crush had lasted for years. Fortunately, he didn't know how she'd pined for him, craving his attention, wanting him to just look at her, acknowledge her…

It was embarrassing. *She* was embarrassing.

She'd thought the years in Chicago had changed her.

She'd thought she'd conquered her demons—the insecurity, the poor self-esteem—but here she was on her wedding day, in her wedding gown, alone.

It was almost laughable.

Her worst fears, her very worst fears, had just come true.

As she reached the top step, the dark stained arched doors opened, and guests poured into the crisp late autumn afternoon, voices, whispers, nervous laughter.

Not all voices were hushed though. There were a few that were loud and sharp and they carried on the breeze with the surging crowd.

"Can't believe it. A wedding without a bride or groom."

"I knew something was wrong when the service didn't start on time."

"What a waste of time. I wish I hadn't bought a new dress for this. I'm hoping I can still return the gift!"

Jenny flinched at the last, recognizing Carol Bingley's strident voice. But then, it was hard not to. Carol Bingley, Marietta's town gossip, had never been particularly fond of the Wright family, or the three blonde Wright girls, saying quite cuttingly a decade ago that 'it was a shame those three Wright girls were all wrong.'

As Carol marched towards Jenny, her stout figure swathed in an appalling yellow, turquoise, and black print, Jenny's sense of self-preservation kicked it. It was time for fight, or flight, and there was no way she could fight Carol here, with others watching.

Jenny fled.

It was the coward's way but she was ashamed, deeply ashamed, and a latent survival instinct drove her back down the church's steps, across the pavement to the street. But once she was on Church Avenue, Jenny kept running, racing to the corner of First and turning right, cutting between homes that were a mix of residential and commercial before reaching Crawford Avenue and then on to historic Bramble Lane.

It was on Bramble Lane, with its treasure-trove of sprawling Victorian and Queen Anne homes, that she slowed.

She loved Bramble Lane. It was like a storybook street and her favorite street in all of Marietta.

She remembered the first time she actually rode her bike down this street. She was in second grade and she'd just gone to the library and returned books and instead of going straight home, she decided to go see all the big pretty houses. She'd seen them before, from the car, but had never explored the street on her own.

She rode slowly, wonderingly down the quiet tree lined street, awed. Dazzled.

This was where the rich people lived. This is where little girls who studied ballet and took piano lessons lived. She could even see a big piano in one of the bay windows.

Her house was so small you couldn't even put a grand piano in the living room. First, it wouldn't fit through the front door. And second, it'd take up the entire room.

There'd be no place for a couch or the TV, and her dad needed both—bad.

No, her house was the size of a matchbox compared to these two- and three-story homes. A few of the houses, like the gorgeous Bramble House, were built of mellow red brick with doors and windows trimmed in thick, white, glossy woodwork, while others were Victorians, ornamented with lavish latticework, asymmetrical turrets, and colorful paint. Regardless of the style, every home at the south end of Bramble Lane was situated on a half acre or more, and had gardens and gates and big front porches with wicker chairs and flower pots.

From second grade on, Jenny desperately wanted to live in one of these beautiful houses. The houses looked perfect, and good, and to Jenny, it seemed only good things could happen inside such elegant walls.

In houses like these, daddies didn't drink too much and yell and break things because they'd drunk too much.

In big beautiful houses mommies wouldn't take to their bed and cry so hard they'd get headaches which meant they couldn't make dinner or put their children to bed because their head hurt.

Jenny was in kindergarten the first time she made her sisters' dinner.

She was still making dinner for her two younger sisters until the day she left for Chicago.

She'd never blamed her parents for their family's difficult

circumstances—poor, struggling, unhappy—but Jenny vowed when she left Marietta, that she'd never ever let herself become like her mother. Dependent on a man. Helpless without him and yet miserable with him.

Nearly limping from the rub of raw blisters, Jenny walked carefully, trying not to aggravate the tender skin more than necessary, trying not to think because really, how could she think? It was impossible to process that today had finally arrived, the day she'd spent months and months planning for, only to have all her dreams collapse.

It was shocking. Shattering. She still couldn't believe it was over. Couldn't believe that Charles had refused to marry her, throwing her family's weaknesses in her face, throwing the things about her that she couldn't change, reducing her to a weakness, too. As if her parents' struggles were all that she was… all that she could be.

Jenny ground her teeth together.

He was wrong. Not just about Jenny, but about her parents too, because both her mother and father had struggled, but they finally got help, going to counseling and attending meetings and coming out stronger and more committed to their marriage than ever before. She was proud of them, fiercely proud.

She drew a slow, deep breath, trying to ease the wild staccato of her heart.

She wished she hadn't run from the church.

She wished she'd gone to the church's parish hall, where

she'd dressed in the side room with the help of her sisters and bridesmaids. She should have headed there and waited for her sisters and friends, because they would have returned eventually to collect their purses and street clothes. If she'd thought clearly, logically, she wouldn't be on yet another street corner, with blistered feet and no money or phone.

An engine sounded behind her, a loud engine that was almost familiar. She stepped back and turned to Colton Thorpe's rusty red truck drawing alongside her.

"Where are you going, darlin'?" Colton asked, pulling to a stop next to her, and rolling down his window.

Ambivalent emotion rushed through her. Years ago she couldn't get him to talk to her, and now he was talking and she didn't want the attention.

But she needed to get home. She needed out of this dress, and shoes and veil. He could get her home, too. Stressed, she sucked in her lower lip, chewed it. "I don't know," she confessed.

"Just out walking?" he asked, blue eyes settling on her face.

"Yes."

"It's a nice fall afternoon."

"It is," she agreed, thinking this was the most ludicrous conversation, but it was better than saying anything that was real or important. Better than crying. Better than falling apart. She couldn't fall apart in public. Couldn't let anyone, much less Colton Thorpe, see her pain.

But conversation seemed to stall out there and as silence stretched, Jenny's heart pounded.

Her world had just turned upside down. And a strange crazy sixth sense whispered that for reasons she didn't yet understand, her world would never be the same.

Jenny swallowed hard and looked at Colton. His gaze met hers. Held.

His eyes were blue.

Strange.

Lots of people had blue eyes. Charles had blue eyes, too. But not like this. Colton's were a deep brilliant marine blue.

Denim blue.

She knew a lot of things about Colton Thorpe. Knew he'd struggled in high school. Knew he'd gone from gangly pre-adolescent to a hot-headed teenager, quick with his fists. Jenny's parents hadn't approved of him. Most parents hadn't approved of him, not with his dangerous reputation for fast driving, fighting, and ruining good girls. Colton left town the day after graduating from Marietta High, wasting no time in finding bigger, greener pastures, and at the same time, leaving a string of broken hearts behind.

She remembered all that, but she didn't remember his blue eyes. Or how square his jaw looked with a little bit of stubble. Or the slightly raised scar on his left cheekbone.

His dirty blonde hair was darker now, more golden brown than blonde, and long enough to hang over his collar. If he wore a collar. Instead he wore a thin cotton t-shirt that stretched tautly over his big shoulders, the soft gray fabric hugging the planes of his broad chest and clinging to his thick biceps.

Colton Thorpe wasn't a teenager, wasn't a kid, wasn't a city sophisticate, either.

He was a man. A big, tough, tough, hard, man with muscles and a piercing blue gaze that made her suddenly doubt everything she knew, and everything she believed.

Her heart did a funny little beat, a sickening one-two, that made her long to sit down, put her head between her knees.

"You feeling all right, darlin'?" Colton asked.

Jenny licked her lower lip. It was dry, so dry, like her mouth and throat. Her heart continued to pound. Her head swam. She was feeling faint, but she couldn't admit it. Jenny Wright was nothing if not professional, having spent far too many years as an executive assistant, working with prickly management, solving difficult problems, putting out real or perceived fires, to fall apart at the drop of a hat. "I'm fine."

He waited a moment before asking, "Do you live here on Bramble Lane?"

"No."

"Going some place on Bramble?"

Her throat ached. "No."

"Where's your car?"

"I don't have one. Not here. My car is in Chicago." She averted her face, hating how her eyes pickled and burned.

She couldn't cry. She must not cry. Charles despised tears, and he'd taught her that she wasn't allowed to cry. He viewed tears as a weakness, and manipulative, and his executive team needed to exude strength and confidence at all times, because Charles Monmouth succeeded where others failed.

She glanced down as rust and crackling brown leaves danced before her and swirled into the street. "The other Windy City," she added, huskily. "It's home. Now."

"A big city girl… but you once lived here?"

"Born at Marietta Regional Hospital. Graduated from Marietta High. So yes, Montana born and raised."

"So where are you staying now?" Colton asked. "With your family?"

She nodded. "I've been at my parents. But tonight I was supposed to be at The Graff Hotel. That's where my things are now."

"Let me take you to the Graff then."

She pictured the old Graff Hotel, Marietta's first hotel, a hotel that had burned down in 1912 and was then rebuilt and reopened with great fanfare in 1914. For three quarters of a century, the hotel had been the spot for weddings, graduations, reunions, and special events until it fell into disrepair. The hotel was closed in the mid seventies, and officially condemned in 1982 and for twenty years it sat, boarded up, a hulking giant, waiting for demolition. But instead of a wrecking ball, one of the Sheenan brothers who'd left Marietta, bought the former landmark and poured millions into renovating the property. The Graff Hotel had only reopened this summer, in time for the tourist season, and Jenny had been so excited to have her reception in the hotel's stunning ballroom.

But now there was no reception. No beautiful dinner banquet. No dancing. No round tables of eight, each with a beautiful fresh floral arrangement costing sixty-five dollars each.

Her heart fell, taking her stomach with it.

All that money. Wasted. All her savings. Gone.

My God.

Such waste. Sickening. Horrifying.

Charles had no idea that she'd paid for the wedding herself. He had no idea that she'd used all of her savings, and filled up every credit card she had, to make today possible, including taking out a new line of credit just to cover her dress.

Charles thought her parents had paid for everything. It's what the bride's family was supposed to do. And she wanted him to think well of her family. She'd wanted him to approve of them. But of course her family didn't have the means to give her the gorgeous wedding Charles Monmouth would expect, and so she paid for it herself. And would be paying for it, for a very long time in the future.

"Can't go there," she murmured. Charles and his family were staying at the Graff, along with sixty of their dearest friends. The Monmouths had chartered two jets to fly everyone in from Chicago, landing at Bozeman, and then shuttling all to Marietta in a caravan of limousines and town cars.

She shuddered at the idea of bumping into Charles, or one of his family now. It would be excruciating to see them, or have to make small talk. What would she say? How could she explain? She didn't understand herself.

No, she'd collect her things from the Graff later. Better to wait until after the Monmouths had decamped from Marietta, and she was fairly certain they'd be flying out soon, today. There was no way they'd linger in town now, not after everything that had happened. "It's probably best to go to my parents' house," she said. "I can figure everything out once I'm there."

"Good idea," he agreed, leaning across to open the door from the inside. "Climb in."

The door squeaked in protest as it opened.

Her gaze dropped to his battered, rusting truck that was somewhere between pumpkin and tomato. "You're sure it runs?" she asked, teasing him, because she knew this was his dad's truck. Tricia said Colton was committed to keeping it running in memory of their father.

He grinned, and patted the scratched metal dash. "Like a champ."

She smiled. She liked his sense of humor. "And that from local hero Colt Thorpe means something."

He looked startled. "You know who I am?"

"Everyone in Marietta does. You're Colton Thorpe, national bull riding champ and Marietta's very own hero."

Colton exhaled hard and made a face. "Darlin', not a hero. Not even close," he protested, before giving the leather bench seat a light pat. "But hop in, and I will get you safely home. I may not be a hero, I can at least pretend to be a gentleman."

CHAPTER THREE

COLTON WATCHED HER settle her shimmering skirts on his torn and cracked leather bench seat. She looked like a goddess in his father's 1941 GMC pickup. His dad had loved this truck and so whenever Colton came home, he made a point of driving it to keep it running, and Colton couldn't help thinking his dad must be smiling now. His dad always did believe a gorgeous girl looked even better in a great pickup truck.

"Where to?" he asked her.

"North Marietta."

He lifted a brow. "*North*?"

She reached up and tugged off the veil and tiara pinned to the top of her golden hair. Wispy tendrils fell from the elaborate chignon to frame her face. And what a face it was. She was so beautiful she made him hurt.

"Chance Avenue," she said, settling the tiara and veil in her lap. "It's over between Second and—"

"I know where it is," he interrupted. "I grew up on Chance, too."

"I know." Her voice was soft, subdued. Her long black

lashes lifted, and for a split second her gaze met his before falling. She smoothed her full skirts, pressing them down over her knees. "We were neighbors."

He frowned. "We were?"

"Your sister Tricia and I were in the same grade, and friends."

"I don't remember you."

She looked at him again, expression wry. "I was a skinny little blonde kid, and four years behind you in school. I think I was in eighth grade when you were a senior in high school so I don't expect you to remember me. It's not as if you paid Tricia's girlfriends any attention." Her lips curved, and a dimple flashed at the corner of her mouth. "You were too busy seducing all the big girls in town."

He stared at a delicate gold wisp clinging to her high cheekbone, drawing attention to her full lips. He loved her lips and the way they curved up, equally smitten with the dimple flashing sweetly, mischievously, at the corner of her mouth. "I wasn't," he said.

"You were. You most absolutely were," she answered firmly, the dimple deepening as she fought a smile. "You had a terrible reputation, Colton—"

"All right. I did." He shifted uncomfortably, uncomfortable because he wanted to touch this beautiful girl, wanted to kiss her full soft mouth and put his tongue where that dimple flashed and everything in him felt unsettled and fierce and yet damn protective, too.

Some asshole had hurt her today.

Some asshole abandoned her when he should be promising to love and protect her.

But what did he know? Lisa claimed he was an asshole, too. It'd been two years since they divorced and yet it was still damn confusing. Not the divorce part. He knew why they were divorced—his beautiful ex-wife loved money, needed money, far more than she loved and needed him—but the fact that he'd fallen in love with her in the first place still blew his mind.

How could he have not seen who she was?

Unfortunately, he knew the answer to that one, too.

He'd fallen for Lisa's beautiful face, hot body, and sexy, husky laugh, not realizing that the seductive smile and rockin' bod didn't mean she had a warm, loving heart.

No, her rockin' bod and beautiful face weren't even his all that long. Lisa filed for divorce just before their fifth wedding anniversary. She remarried the moment the divorce came through to a Tulsa gentleman thirty years her senior and one hundred times richer.

The only good thing to come out of the marriage was the fact that they never had kids.

It would have killed Colton to have a baby and then put that child through an ugly divorce.

Eager to close the door on the past, Colton held out his hand to the princess perched on the bench seat next to him. "I'm Colton Thorpe," he said gruffly. "And you are… ?"

"Jenny Wright," she answered, blushing as she put her hand in his.

His strong fingers closed around her palm. The moment her palm pressed to his, skin to skin, he felt a quiver in her, like a current of pure unadulterated energy.

Just as quickly desire surged through him, hot hungry heat filling his veins and blood pooling behind the zipper of his jeans. It was all he could do not to fidget. This beautiful girl was friends with his sister? "Jenny Wright," he repeated, releasing her hand.

She nodded, tucking her fingers into her full tulle skirt.

"And you grew up on Chance Avenue," he said, putting his hand on the stick shift.

"Yes. Same block as you, same side. Fifth house down."

It had been too many years. He couldn't picture her house. "Which one?"

She swallowed hard. "The blue one."

The blue one.

That's all he needed to know, because he knew her house right away. There had only been one blue house on the street, and the little blue house, her house, looked as if it would topple from the foundations any minute.

His family had struggled. They'd gone without trips, dinners out, and new cars. But compared to the Wrights, the Thorpes had lived like kings.

JENNY SAW HIS shock before he could hide it, his black lashes swiftly lowering to conceal his surprise.

He shifted into drive and pulled away the curb. Jenny's hands knotted, fingers clenching around the handle of her bouquet.

Even among poor people there were standards. Jenny's family had been the poorest on the block.

Poverty scared people. People acted like it was contagious, and no one wanted to catch being poor.

But Jenny had helped distance herself from her humble past by pretending to be someone other than Jenny Wright. She'd learned to wear the right clothes, apply the right makeup, to present herself as if she mattered. Because she did matter.

"I appreciate the ride," she said, watching the scenery as he traveled west down Bramble. The big houses grew more modest, transitioning from two story homes to cozy craftsman and turn of the century bungalows.

"My pleasure," he answered.

Something had changed between them, she thought. He'd grown quiet. He was thinking, and that worried her. But then, right now, everything worried her.

"It would have been a long walk home," she added, trying to fill the silence, even as she struggled to ignore his energy.

There was a lot of energy crackling around him, but then there always had been.

Even as a teenager Colton was larger than life. And now as a man, Colton wasn't just a big personality, but a dominant man. At six-two, he was solid, with broad shoulders and a thick chest, with carved biceps and long muscular legs wrapped in soft faded denim.

She drew a quick, nervous breath and fidgeted with her flowers, senses stirred, imagination overwrought.

She'd pined for him when she was younger, and she'd been just a little girl. It hadn't been sexual. Her crush was far more innocent than that. But she'd been drawn to him, intrigued by him, wanting to be part of his circle and world.

She could still see herself in sixth grade, playing at Tricia's house, lying on Tricia's floor, pretending to sketch houses and clothes and other pretty things, but from the corner of her eye she'd watch Colton come and go from his room in various stages of dress and undress—and it was all she could do not to stare.

It was all she could do to remember to keep breathing.

It was all she could do to remember to keep breathing now.

Because every breath made her nose and senses tingle. He smelled so good. His cologne or aftershave or whatever it was he wore made her pulse jump and her insides weak. The scent was nice. He smelled rich, warm and seductively spicy. Like a man.

Like a man should.

Charles also wore a scent but it didn't suit him. It was

too strong for him, and bold, and a mix of citrus and floral like something you'd smell on a magazine advertisement.

Just thinking of Charles made her go cold.

How could Charles do this to her today?

She didn't understand. Or maybe she did and was just in denial.

Jenny Wright might look like a princess in an expensive designer wedding gown, but underneath the gown she was still white trash.

Her eyes pickled. Her stomach burned.

She lifted her bouquet to her nose, inhaling the freesias tucked into the orange roses and rust dahlias, trying to hide her hurt. The flowers were sweet, and she inhaled again, needing something good, because she felt bad. Really, really bad. She'd failed her family. Failed herself.

The shock hadn't worn off, but shame was creeping in, as well as reality. There were so many things that needed to be done. Someone would have to call The Graff Hotel's catering department. Someone would have to let the staff know there would be no reception. She wondered who had done it. Charles's mom? One of Jenny's sisters? Charles himself?

Jenny squeezed her eyes closed, trying not to think of her lovely five-tiered wedding cake, and all the bottles of champagne that Charles's family had flown in with them...

Her insides lurched, and her heart just kept falling. Free-falling, a terrible plummeting sensation that made her want to curl up in a ball and hide.

"Pigtails." Colton said suddenly, breaking the silence. "White-blond pigtails. In French braids."

She looked up, saw his frown of concentration.

"Was that you?" he demanded.

She nodded.

The edge of his lips lifted. "And you were skinny. Your knees and shoulders were huge."

He glanced at her for confirmation.

She nodded again.

"I called you Bones," he added after a moment. "And if memory serves, I think I made you cry. More than once."

"You did," she agreed.

He shot her an apologetic glance. "I felt bad when you cried. I'm sorry."

"It's fine. I was really skinny back then."

"You're not bony anymore."

She laughed at his deadpan tone. She liked the way he delivered a line. It was dry and clever. He was clever. And the fact that he had a sense of humor was a relief. Charles didn't laugh. Charles took himself very seriously. "I filled out late in high school. The Wright girls are all late bloomers."

"There are more of you?"

"I have two younger sisters. They still live here in Marietta."

"They didn't want to move?"

"It costs money to move."

Silence fell. She'd obviously killed the conversation with that zinger.

Good job, Jen.

She lifted her flowers again, burying her nose in the bouquet to hide the sheen of tears.

She would not cry. She wouldn't. Not here, not now. *Come on, Jen. Pull it together.*

And then suddenly before she knew it, they were bumping across the tracks and then continuing through a neighborhood of small blocks of small, plain houses. These streets weren't lined with trees. The houses didn't have pretty painted fences or wrought iron. Most fences were chain link and a pretty flower garden was an oddity, not the norm. But then, Montana winters were long and snow often lingered until late May or early June, so there was little point pouring one's energy into a garden that would just get buried again come October.

It wouldn't be long now until they reached her house.

Her stomach rose and fell. Her hands shook.

What would she say to her parents? How was she to explain this? She'd worked for Charles's company for over five years and had been his girlfriend for the past three.

And then they arrived. Colton braked in front of the Wrights' low, squat blue house with its sagging front porch and a composite roof that looked almost like a patchwork quilt with its pieces of pink-gray asphalt against the faded brown and slate.

She turned away from the house, and gathered her skirt, and flowers, and managed a smile. "Thank you so very much for the ride. I really appreciate it."

He opened his door, and came around to the passenger side, and open her door for her. "My pleasure," he said.

She slid out, careful not to tear the delicate tulle on the cracked leather bench seat. On the sidewalk she let her full skirts drop. "It was nice to see you again, Colton, and you'll have to give Tricia my love. And um…you can—" she broke off, frowned, struggled to find the words, "—tell her," she said, "what happened, if you want." She saw his expression and added quickly, "Tricia was there today. At the church. She was one of my guests. I'm sure she'll be curious."

He made a rough sound in the back of his throat. "I'm not going to tell her anything. And it's okay if she's curious. Let people be curious. You don't owe them an explanation."

"I do—" she broke off, frowned. "Don't I?"

"They already know the wedding didn't happen. What more do they need to know?"

Everything, she thought, painfully familiar with how small towns thrived on gossip. It's one of the reasons she'd left Marietta after completing two years of community college in Bozeman. She didn't want people talking about her, and they couldn't talk about her if they didn't know who she was, which is why Chicago had appealed. It was a big city, far from Marietta, and even though the Chicago temp agency warned Jenny that it was unlikely that she'd find a desirable job in corporate America due to her lack of skills, Jenny proved the agency wrong. She'd shown them that anyone could do anything if you worked hard enough.

"True," she said, but so unconvincingly that Colton's eyebrow lifted.

She made a face. "They're going to talk," she added.

"So?"

"I hate it when people talk."

"Some folks have nothing better to do than talk, but it shouldn't bother you. You don't answer to other people. They don't own you, or control you, so you shouldn't care what they think."

She nearly ducked her head. "I'm just… private."

"Me, too. But being private doesn't mean others won't gossip." He studied her a moment. "Sounds like it's time you toughened up. Grew some thick skin. Otherwise, darlin', you aren't going to survive this life. Beautiful and fragile make a pretty ornament on a Christmas tree but not for every day living."

Jenny didn't like that at all. "I'm not beautiful and fragile. I'm pretty tough, actually."

"Is that so?"

"Yes. I may not look like a Montana girl in this fancy gown, but I'm no innocent. I've been around the block before and you're right, life can play rough, but so can I." And then she marched up the steps to her childhood home, head high, shoulders squared to prove the point.

Jenny Wright wasn't a fragile, decorative little thing.

Jenny Wright was Montana born.

She had guts. And grit. And no man was going to define her. Not now. Not ever.

Chapter Four

COLTON WATCHED JENNY climb the steps of her house, her gently rounded hips swaying with every step up the sagging wooden stairs to her front door as if she were Cinderella returning home after the ball.

He felt a strange ache in his chest as she opened the unlocked front door and disappeared inside the house without a backward glance.

Gone.

As she should be.

This was her home, her family, this is where she belonged.

And yet…

And yet…

No, he couldn't go there. He didn't need complications. He was a traveling man, a man who needed nothing more than his leather duffel and his truck. Women didn't belong on the road, certainly not pretty little blonde things like Jenny Wright.

But he was disappointed when the door closed behind her. He liked looking at her. She was easy on the eyes and damn hard on his self-control.

Returning to his truck, though, Colton wondered at her life in Chicago. What kind of man would leave his woman at the church on her wedding day? What kind of man would abandon his woman just when she was feeling safe?

A man who was no man at all, he thought, shaking his head, disgusted.

Colton drove home and parked in front of his house. His sister's car, a silver Jeep Cherokee, was in the driveway. Tricia was back.

He entered the house through the kitchen door. His mom and sister were in the kitchen, his mom in her wheelchair at the table, with Tricia at the stove, in a pretty teal cocktail dress and heels, boiling water for tea.

"Apparently he changed his mind," Tricia said, lifting the whistling kettle off the hot burner. "Nobody knows exactly why, but Carol Bingley said Charles realized that Jenny was marrying him for his money—"

"*What*?" Colton demanded, tossing his cowboy hat onto the kitchen table and turning to face his sister.

"I was just telling Mom about the wedding I went to this afternoon," Tricia said, dropping tea bags into the two mugs on the counter. "We sat around for a half-hour waiting for Jen and Charles to put in an appearance and then abruptly Charles showed up and said the wedding was off, and that was that—" she glanced at Colton. "Do you want tea?"

He shook his head. "No. And that's a terrible thing to

say about your friend."

Tricia made a face. "I didn't say it. Carol Bingley said it."

"What's terrible is that you'd repeat it."

"I don't believe it. Everyone knows Mrs. Bingley is the worst gossip ever, but Mom wanted to know what happened, so I was giving her all the details." Tricia filled the mugs with hot water and looked at her mom. "You should have come today, Mom. It was certainly interesting, and you were invited."

Mrs. Thorpe folded her hands in her lap. "It's not easy getting around in my wheelchair."

"Colt said he'd help you," Tricia answered, placing the tea kettle back on the stove and glancing at her brother. "I could have sworn she invited you, too, you know. At least, she asked me for your address."

"I didn't get an invite," he said shortly. But even if he'd received one, he probably hadn't even opened the envelope. Colton avoided weddings like the plague. So not his thing. "And why is Mrs. Bingley gossiping about Jenny in the first place? Jenny hasn't lived here for years."

Tricia shrugged. "The wedding was a big deal, not just here, but in Chicago. Their engagement was written up in all the papers—he's old Chicago money, so their wedding was this big society thing—and apparently some Chicago lifestyle magazine was doing a big glossy feature on the Montana wedding. They even flew a writer and photographer out to cover it. Mrs. Bingley was talking about that quite a bit, too."

"It's all so stupid," Colton retorted, leaning against the counter and folding his arm over his big chest, the fabric tight across his shoulders. "Weddings should be about the bride and groom, not society."

Tricia shot him an arch look. "If I recall, your wedding seven years ago was the wedding of the year in Tulsa."

He made a rough sound. "Like I said, weddings should be about the bride and groom, not the parents, not the family, not society. A wedding is two people making a huge commitment to each other, and that's personal. And private."

"I take it when you get married next time you're having a very small wedding?" Tricia teased, carrying the steaming mugs to the table, placing one in front of her mother before sitting down with the other.

"Not getting married again," he said shortly. "I'll bed a woman but I'm not going to be her ATM."

"Colton!" Mrs. Thorpe exclaimed. "I won't tolerate rude talk and crass behavior in my home."

"Sorry, Mom." His big shoulders shifted, biceps bunching. "But I've learned my lesson. Not going down the path again."

Tricia gave him a sympathetic glance. "You didn't know Lisa was so material—"

"How did we even get onto this subject?" He demanded. "It's not my favorite subject. We were talking about Jenny."

He hesitated a moment before adding, "And what makes Mrs. Bingley think Jenny was marrying for money?"

Tricia took a second to answer, choosing her words with care. "Jenny is really smart, and practical. She grew up without a lot of security, and it's important to her. She wouldn't marry a man without some… resources. She just wouldn't. She said as much when she left Marietta all those years ago, too."

"That doesn't mean she's a gold digger," he protested, not liking any of this.

"And I never said she was. I'm just repeating Mrs. Bingley's gossip…" Tricia shrugged, lifted her mug, and blew on the steaming surface before looking up at her brother. "But if you saw Charles Monmouth, you'd wonder, too. He might be filthy rich, but he's certainly not much to look at, and Jenny's gorgeous now, Colt. Really gorgeous—"

"I am sure he had good traits besides his bank account," Colton said, cutting her short. "Besides, love is supposed to be blind."

"Definitely in this case." Tricia carefully sipped her tea. "Charles looks like PeeWee Herman. Total goober." She wrinkled her nose. "Sorry if that sounds unkind, but he's definitely not my type. Not that my love life is anything to brag about." She looked from her mother to her brother. "But regarding Jenny, I'm on her side. I don't blame her for choosing security and stability over handsome and sexy—"

"Don't want to hear any more." Colton pushed off the

counter, unable and unwilling to listen to another word. There really was too much gossip in Marietta. But wasn't that always the curse of small towns? He crossed to his mother, dropped a kiss on the top of her head. "What time do you want to go out for dinner, Mom?"

"We don't need to go out tonight after all," his mom answered, tilting her head back to look up at him. "Dinner is being delivered."

"It is?" he asked, surprised.

"One of the Wright girls is dropping dinner off. Mandy or Charity. I forget which."

Tricia saw Colton's confused expression and quickly explained, "The prime rib dinner at the Graff Hotel was already prepared and paid for, and Mandy knew Jenny would hate to have it wasted so she's organizing meals, and promised to drop us off dinner for the three of us on her way back home tonight."

Colton couldn't imagine a worse dinner. "We're eating the wedding leftovers?"

"Not leftovers. The reception was cancelled, and there is food for one hundred and fifty. It's a prime rib dinner, too, Colton," his mother said. "From The Graff."

"I understand that," he answered, opening the refrigerator and looking for something cold to drink. A beer would be perfect right now but the only cold drinks were his mother's cans of Ensure. He closed the refrigerator door, and ran his palm over his jaw, feeling trapped, thinking Grey's

Saloon sounded like the perfect place to be right now. "But I thought I was taking you out, Mom."

"There's no need to go out if we can eat a nice meal in," his mom answered.

"Mandy's going to a lot of trouble delivering all these dinners, too," Tricia added. "The least we can do is eat the meal she's delivering."

Colton knew better than to argue with two women at one time, especially if they were his mom and sister. "Fine. We'll eat here, and I'll take you out another night. I'm here for a week. We have plenty of time to visit the Diner." He leaned past his mom, reached for his hat and jammed it on his head. "And since dinner isn't here, I'm going to head over to Grey's and have a beer or two. I'll be back in a couple hours."

And then he was walking out the kitchen door before his sister or mom could stop him.

He needed fresh air, a strong drink, and some non-chatty male company because it made him sick to think that beautiful Jenny Wright might have actually been marrying this Charles guy for his money.

JENNY WAS GRATEFUL when Chelsea and Sage appeared at her front door, with her suitcase from the hotel, and her clothes and makeup from the parish hall. They'd come to rescue her, they told her, after greeting her parents, and giving her hugs.

Jenny didn't need rescuing, but she did need to get out. She needed her friends, too. Chelsea and Sage had been close friends since high school, although Chelsea and Sage had been friends long before that, having gone to the same elementary school while Jenny attended Park Elementary on the opposite side of town. Park Elementary was also a bit of a euphemism, as directly across from the school's playground was a gun store, a liquor store, and a gas station catering to the truckers.

In Marietta, the wrong side of the tracks was literally the wrong side of the tracks.

But now she and Sage and Chelsea were out, having taken over one of the booths at the back of Grey's Saloon and drinking Cosmos in short tumblers because that's how they did it at Grey's.

Fortunately, Reese was there behind the bar tonight, and he made the drinks extra strong, having heard all about the non-wedding wedding event from other customers earlier.

"It's going to be okay," Jenny said for what must have been the fifth time since arriving at Grey's Saloon with Sage and Chelsea a half-hour ago. "Everything will be fine," she added firmly, as if saying so would make it true. "I'll find a new job and settle in and soon all this will be behind me."

"You're going to stay in Chicago then?" Sage asked, her wrinkled brow revealing her misgivings.

"I'm happy there," Jenny answered. She saw Sage and

Chelsea exchanged dubious glances. "I am," she insisted. "It's familiar now. I'm comfortable there."

"It's also expensive," Chelsea said. "Money goes a lot farther here."

Jenny rubbed her thumb across the moisture beading her tumbler. The drink was good and strong and it was warming her nicely. She wasn't a big drinker but the vodka was easing the chill inside her. It'd been brutal at home, facing her parents, explaining that Charles had changed his mind and she didn't know why, but she had to believe it was for the best.

Maybe it was.

Maybe it wasn't.

She was just glad she hadn't cried while apologizing to them. She hadn't crumpled. She'd stood tall, and her voice had been firm, and she'd kissed her parents, and hugged them.

Jenny may have been calm, but her mom had been emotional, pressing trembling fingers to her mouth, while tears welled in her eyes. "Did we do something wrong, baby?" her mother had asked.

"Heavens no," Jenny answered briskly, hugging her mother again. "This was between Charles and me. This was an us thing, not a you thing, and I'm sorry for the embarrassment I've caused. I'm sorry to disappoint you, too. I know you both were so excited and proud."

Thank goodness the doorbell rang then. Chelsea and

Sage arrived in the nick of time. They'd changed from their bridesmaid gowns into street clothes and had unpinned and combed out their hair, losing the formal wedding up-dos.

"We figured you didn't need to bump into the Monmouths again today," Chelsea said, setting the suitcase in the hall.

"And you probably would like to get out of the dress," Sage added. "So we brought clothes." She held up a little gold bag. "And chocolates."

Of course Sage would bring chocolates. Sage, owner of Copper Mountain Chocolates, knew Jenny had a terrible weakness for salted caramels and dark decadent chocolate. Jenny smiled through her tears. "Thank you."

"Now go change," Chelsea said. "We're dragging you out for a drink. And even if you don't need one, we do. We want to know what's going on."

At Grey's Saloon, in the back booth in the dark bar, Jenny told them everything. Or virtually everything. She left out the part about meeting Colton Thorpe, and running down the street, and then the ride home in Colton's truck…

"Don't leave," Chelsea said more firmly. "You belong here. This is home."

Jenny pushed back a long blonde lock of hair, tucking it behind her ear. "What would I do here?"

"Do what you do in Chicago… administrative stuff. Assistant to the manager sort of thing." Chelsea thought for a moment. "I wonder if the school district office could use you. You should check on Monday and see if they have any openings."

"I'm sure there would be something in Bozeman," Sage said.

"But that's a forty-minute drive," Chelsea protested. "She won't want to do that, especially in winter. She might as well live in Bozeman then, which actually isn't a terrible idea. Bozeman would probably be easier for you, if you've gotten used to city living, and they have the university there, and lots of big corporations..." Her voice drifted away, her attention caught by something happening at the front of the bar.

Jenny turned to look to see what Chelsea was looking at, and her heart did a funny double beat.

Colton Thorpe had arrived.

Heat surged through her, blood scalding her cheeks. Feeling terribly juvenile and breathless, she watched as he crossed the saloon and took a seat at the long bar counter.

"Wow," Sage said.

Chelsea watched Jenny watching Colton. "Didn't you used to have a huge crush on Colton?" she asked, trying to suppress a smirk and failing. Probably deliberately failing, too. "Back when we were in high school?"

STILL HOT, CHEEKS still burning, Jenny shook her head hard. "*No.*"

Chelsea's smirk grew. "Yes, you did. You did. And it was *bad.*"

"No, not in high school," Jenny said, tugging on her black sweater, ridiculously overwarm. "Maybe in sixth grade. Seventh grade. Back when I was just a kid and didn't know better."

CHAPTER FIVE

SHOULDERS HUNCHED, COLTON propped his elbows on the bar and glared at his beer bottle.

He was angry. He felt cheated. Robbed.

He came to Grey's Saloon for a cold drink and some proper male conversation—small talk about crops and ranching, weather and how it impacted local crops and ranchers, as well as speculation about tomorrow's NFL games.

What he didn't come for was female chatter and laughter. And he certainly didn't drive to Grey's Saloon to be around Jenny Wright.

He was here to escape thoughts of Jenny Wright.

But even at the counter he could hear her and her friends in the back booth talking. She was with one of the Carrigan girls... one of Dani's younger sisters. He'd gone to school with Dani. They'd been in the same class. He'd kissed her their freshman year of high school at a party. Seven minutes in heaven or something like that. And then the seven minutes became fourteen. She wouldn't let it go further than that. But of course he had to try.

He shook his head, glad he wasn't a kid anymore. He'd sure gotten into a lot of trouble as a kid. He'd learned a few things since then, things like self-control.

But when Jenny's voice rose in husky laughter from the back of the bar, Colton felt a tightness in his chest and an impatience in his pulse that was the opposite of control.

He was attracted to Jenny. He wanted her. But she was exactly the kind of woman he shouldn't want because she seemed to be an awful lot like his ex-wife…

A beautiful blonde in need of a sugar daddy.

His stomach rolled. He took a long swig of beer. From now on he was keeping Jenny at arm's length. She might be easy on the eyes, but she was totally off limits.

JENNY WAS DETERMINED to ignore Colton. She refused to look at him. Wouldn't even peek in his direction. He wasn't here.

Well, he *was* here, and drinking beer, was on his second right now.

Not that she was counting. Or paying him any attention. Or had noticed that he'd changed from his t-shirt to a long-sleeved Henley that hugged his muscular torso like a glove.

"He's the honorary chair this year for the rodeo," Sage said, ever so casually, as if reading Jenny's mind.

Jenny sipped her cocktail. "Who?" she asked innocently, feigning ignorance.

Chelsea's lips curved as she curled in the corner of her side of the booth. "You're not fooling anyone. You've glanced at him at least a half-dozen times in the past half hour."

"I don't even know what you're talking about," Jenny protested, her hands circling her cocktail glass, her finger strangely empty since removing her ring at her parents' house.

Sage shook her head. "You always were a terrible liar."

"Horrendous," Chelsea agreed, lifting her cocktail in mock salute. "But that's okay. It's good to know that in a world of rapid change, some things are the same."

Jenny glared at them. "I thought you two were supposed to be my friends."

"We are," Sage said. "That's why we're giving you some need-to-know-information."

"Colton Thorpe's a big deal now," Chelsea added. "The steering committee was thrilled when he agreed to be the chair for this year's rodeo."

"Why this year?" Jenny asked, hoping to distract them.

"It's the seventy-fifth anniversary this year," Sage explained, "and who better to represent the Copper Mountain Rodeo than Marietta's—" she stopped and glanced at Chelsea, then Jenny, uncertain. Her worried expression turned to a frown. "Um… Jenny… Charles has just walked in…" Her frown deepened. "And he's, uh, not walking so good."

Stomach falling, Jenny turned in the booth to look. Her stomach fell even further, taking her heart with it. It was Charles. He was still in his tuxedo, too, but now missing the bowtie and with the collar unbuttoned, revealing his throat and pale chest.

In all the years she'd worked for him, she'd never seen Charles publicly disheveled. "What is he doing here?" she whispered, glancing at her watch. Shouldn't he have left Marietta hours ago?

Charles spotted them in the back corner. He staggered towards them.

Oh, God. He *was* drunk. But Charles never drank too much. It was one of his top three cardinal rules.

"Apparently he's looking for you" Sage said.

Icy cold replaced the dizzying warmth Jenny felt when Colton entered the bar and she slouched low in the booth, wishing the ground would open up. She did not want to talk to Charles. Not now. Not ever. "I can't do this," she said, her voice low and hoarse. "Can't listen to any more from him."

"If that's what you want, we'll get rid of him," Chelsea said, sitting tall and straightening her shoulders, looking every inch the authoritative history teacher she was.

Sage tucked a long red curl behind her ear. "But what if he's come to apologize?" she asked. "What if he changed his mind?"

Before Jenny could respond, Charles's footsteps rang out

on the hardwood floor, and then he was there, swaying next to their table.

"Jenny," he said, slurring her name.

Jenny wrinkled her nose. He reeked. Sweat and alcohol and way too much cologne.

"Jenny," he repeated louder. "I need to speak to you."

Stomach churning, Jenny jerked her chin up to look into his pale blue eyes which were more pink than blue. He didn't just stink, he looked like hell, too. "You're drunk," she said.

"Oh, yeah. I am," he agreed. "Most definitely I am."

She didn't know whether to laugh or feel sorry for him. "How did you get here?"

"Walked." He swayed on his feet. "Got lost. It's a bigger town than I thought."

It wasn't a big town. The Graff Hotel was just two measly blocks away from Grey's Saloon. "You must have gone the wrong direction. If you'd left the hotel entrance and walked down First, you would have been here in less than five minutes."

"Well, I didn't. I went past the depot and then a lumberyard and to some strip mall with a bar called Wolf Den. Definitely not my crowd." He swayed and had to grab the table for support. "Bikers and truckers everywhere. Maybe even a hooker. Hard to say."

Jenny suppressed a laugh. Wolf Den was not a bar for the faint of heart. She couldn't even imagine Charles Monmouth walking in there. In his tux no less. "How much did you drink?"

"Jack Daniels."

"Not what. How much?"

"A whole bottle. I think." He reached up to push lank brown hair back from his forehead. The gesture required tremendous concentration. "Jen, I think I made a mistake. I don't want to lose you—"

"This is just the alcohol talking," she interrupted him, the urge to laugh disappearing. "And I don't like drunks and men who get sloppy on alcohol. But you know that."

"'Cause your dad's a drunk."

Jenny would have smacked Charles if he wasn't already such a mess. Instead she got to her feet and faced him. "Go back to the hotel. Get your stuff. And go home—"

"Not without you, Jen," he protested, reaching for her.

She sidestepped his grab. "No. I'm not going with you. We're finished. You made that perfectly clear earlier—"

"I was wrong."

"No."

"I was. And I'm sorry. Okay? I'm groveling. Want me to kneel?" He looked at her, eyes completely unfocused. "Fine, I'll kneel."

She yanked on his arm to keep him from going to his knees. "This isn't funny, Charles. I'm not amused. Please go. Now."

"I can't. I can't go without you. Come back to Chicago

with me. Come home with me, and we'll just put this behind us. Pretend it didn't happen—"

"But it did happen!" She took a quick step back as he reached for her again. "And I don't want to do this. It's humiliating. For both of us."

"No one's looking." The words ran together, a sloppy slur. "And if they are, who cares? I don't care. This is just a pisspot of a town—"

"Hey!" Chelsea protested, interrupting Charles. "That's rude."

He glanced at her, held his hands up. "Sorry. But it's true." He turned back to Jenny. "So come with me, sweetie, and we'll just put this behind us and pretend it didn't happen."

"But it did happen," Jenny said fiercely. "And Marietta isn't a pisspot. It's my home. It's where all the people I love live, and you shamed me here. You shamed my entire family—"

"They'll get over it."

"Maybe. And maybe not. But you don't have a say in it. You have no say in my life—"

"Sweetie, you're being dramatic."

Jenny laughed, incredulous, her gaze briefly meeting Sage and Chelsea's. "Dramatic? Charles, today was the most painful, embarrassing day of my life. Today was supposed to be our wedding… the wedding we planned for months… and now what do you propose we do? Plan another wedding?

Run off to Vegas?"

"We don't need to get married. There's no reason to marry."

"There's not?"

"No. We're a good team without being married. We work good together. We work damn great together." He was slurring the words but he smacked his hand on his other for emphasis. "Why marry? Why ruin a great thing?"

"Because we wanted a family," she whispered.

He swiped the air with his hand. "Don't need a family. Don't need kids. I don't even like kids. Snotty nosed little bastards always whining and crying for something."

She couldn't believe any of this. "You are out of your mind."

"I'm not. I actually know exactly what I'm saying."

"You do?"

"Yes. I know you're mad, and hurt, but you'll get over it. We'll go back to Chicago and things will be okay."

"They won't."

"Why not?"

"I wanted a family, Charles. I wanted to be a mom."

"Kids will ruin your figure." He grinned at her. "You've a great figure, too."

Jenny felt a bubble of hysterical laughter rise in her chest, making her throat ache and her eyes burn. "You are so drunk you're not even making sense. You need to go back to the hotel and sleep this off—"

"I will, if you come back with me," he said grabbing at her, his fingers wrapping around her arm. "I need you."

"Too late."

"Come on. Don't be mean. We're a team. You and me."

She peeled his fingers off, disgusted. "We were never a team."

He looked injured. "Of course we were. We were the best team. You and me working together, making money, making Charles Monmouth III the best wealth advisor in all of Chicago."

"And let me guess…you don't want to marry me, but you'd still like me to keep working for you?"

"Yes!" His bloodshot eyes lit up. "There's no assistant better than you."

"You're out of your mind."

"You can still live with me. That was good."

"You don't love me. You never loved me," she added softly, wonderingly, realizing all over again how empty and cold their relationship had been.

"I love everything about you." He reached for her again. "Just don't want to marry you. But that's okay. Not everybody needs to settle down and all that."

She slapped his hand as he made another grab for her. "Don't!"

"Sweetie."

"You need to go back to the Graff Hotel. You need to sober up. I'll call you a cab."

"I don't want a cab. I want you. Come home with me."

"No." She blinked hard, her eyes gritty, stinging, her heart on fire, too. Because this was her fault. All of this was her fault. She'd lost herself in Chicago, lost her values and her dreams and had settled for a relationship that had nothing to do with love. "We're finished. It's over. We're through. You need to go back to Chicago, Charles—"

"No."

"*Yes.*" Her voice broke, pain and exhaustion wearing her down, bringing her to an all new low. "Please, go, Charles. Just go." The tears were starting to fall and she couldn't stop them, all dignity and self-respect gone.

"Jenny," Charles protested, making another grab for her and suddenly Colton was there, stepping between them, shifting Jenny behind him.

"The lady said no," Colton's deep voice was hard. His big frame blocked Charles's path, preventing him from having access to her. "Now why don't you do as she said, and take yourself back to the hotel and sober up before you say or do something you just might regret."

Charles squinted up at Colton. "I don't think your name is Jenny, and I don't remember talking to you."

"It's not Jenny. It's Colt Thorpe, and this is Marietta, not Chicago and we don't treat our women this way in Marietta. Understand me?"

Charles drew himself tall, but even then he barely came to Colton's shoulder. "I don't think you know who you're talking to, cowboy."

The corner of Colton's mouth curved, his dark blue eyes sparking. "Oh, I know exactly who I'm talking to." Expression hard, jaw tight, he turned to look at Jenny. "You okay?"

She nodded, and wiped away tears.

"Want me to throw him out?" Colton asked brusquely.

Her eyes met his, and she shook her head. "No."

"I'd be happy to."

Her lips trembled. She wanted so badly to smile. Instead she gulped a breath as her eyes met his. There was heat in his eyes. So much heat. And it wasn't a friendly fire. It was protective as well as intimidating, and it struck her that Colton Thorpe, if provoked, could be a dangerous man.

He'd certainly had made a name for himself as a teenager with his love of fighting. She couldn't imagine that he'd lost any of his speed or strength since then. If anything, he was probably even better with his fists.

"Thank you, but no, that's not necessary," she said. "He might break something," she added. "And his family is lawsuit happy. It's not worth it." She shot Charles a furious, scathing glance. "He's not worth it."

She looked from Charles to her friends who were watching wide-eyed, and then back to Colton's whose brilliant blue gaze burned against the bronze of his skin.

The intensity of Colton's gaze made her legs turn to jelly and her belly flip and her throat seal closed.

There wasn't enough air in the bar.

Wasn't enough air anywhere.

She grabbed her purse from the table and stumbled outside. She paced outside the bar, back and forth on the pavement, her silhouette shadowed from the cascading moonlight, footsteps loud on the quiet night. Marietta could turn into a ghost town at night if there wasn't something special happening downtown.

She shoved hair back from her face as she marched back and forth, trying to work through her chaotic emotions. Today had been such a rollercoaster, and the drops and dips just kept coming, the free-fall feeling getting worse as the night went on.

Charles would keep her as an assistant but wouldn't marry her.

He loved her body but didn't love her.

He hated kids. Had he ever even wanted a family?

What was true? And real? And how could she get it all so wrong?

She rubbed at her temple, head throbbing, eyes stinging, heartsick.

For a smart girl, she'd been so damn stupid…

The bar door opened, yellow light spilled out. Slow, measured footsteps sounded behind her. She glanced over her shoulder, expecting her friends. Instead it was Colton.

Another hot electric jolt shot through her as he stepped behind her. She felt him all the way through her. Madness.

"I told the girls I'd check on you," Colton said quietly.

"They're worried about you."

"I'm fine."

Colton stood with his boots planted, arms crossed over his chest, shoulders a mile wide. "Sorry, darlin'. Nobody is going to believe that one."

She shot him a hard look. "You don't need to be nice to me. I'm not going to break."

"Never said you were."

She shook her head and resumed pacing, fingers balling into fists as she marched back and forth. "I am so mad I can't stand it. So mad I want to scream."

Colton's head tipped sideways as he watched her frenetic pacing. "He's drunk, darlin'. He'll sober up. Tomorrow morning things will be fine—"

"No, they won't," she said, cutting him short. "And I'm glad." She shot him another swift glance, nerves taut, screaming. She felt as if she was about to fall apart and it had nothing to do with Charles showing up at Grey's Saloon drunk. It had nothing to do with Charles at all. "I was stupid. I've been stupid. It's rather horrifying, actually."

"Stupid how?"

"It wasn't enough, and I tried to pretend it was." She clapped a hand to her forehead and pressed hard as if the pressure could silence the wild whir of thoughts and the frantic tangled emotion. "I should have been the one to stop this. I should have been the one to see it for what it was. To name it. Label it. I should have at the very least been *honest*." She pressed harder at her head, holding all the brutal recriminations in. "I wasn't, though. And that's the part I can't forgive. It's not him. It's me."

"People make mistakes."

"Yeah," she choked, looking away, and biting into her lip, unable to say more. As it was she'd said too much.

The door to the bar opened. Chelsea and Sage stepped out, the door closing behind them.

"Hey," Sage said, coming up to give Jenny a hug. "It's going to be okay."

Jenny nodded, and blinked back tears, grateful for the hug, and her friends. She didn't have this in Chicago. She had no one in Chicago. Just her job. And her professional reputation. "Thanks," she murmured against Sage's shoulder.

"It's certainly been an interesting day," Chelsea said, smiling at Jenny and keeping her tone light. "You are going to have *stories*, girl."

Jenny wiped away the tears before they could fall. "I could use a few less stories right now." She drew a deep ragged breath. "Speaking of stories, what's Charles doing?"

"Sleeping," Chelsea answered.

"He passed out," Sage added.

"Passed out?" Jenny repeated.

Sage nodded. "He's out cold."

Chelsea fished in her purse for her car keys. "Reese said he'd let him sleep it off for awhile and then get a cab for him."

Jenny exhaled with relief. She was glad she wouldn't have to deal with Charles. She'd had more than enough of Charles

Monmouth III. "Good."

Chelsea dangled the keys from her finger. "You must be pretty tired, too."

"I am," Jenny agreed, but she wasn't ready to go home. She didn't want to go home. Didn't want to be trapped in her little house with her family worrying about her, fussing over her.

"I'll drive you back," Chelsea offered.

Jenny hesitated. She wanted to go to Chelsea's house. Wanted to go to Sage's. Wanted to go anywhere but to her house. It would be awful. It'd be suffocating. "Sure," she said, unconvincingly.

Sage and Chelsea exchanged glances. "You can come back to my apartment," Sage offered. "I can make a bed up for you on my couch."

Jenny was seriously tempted, but she also knew that Sage had to work in the morning, which meant Sage would need to wake up early to start melting the ingredients and pouring all the gourmet chocolates she made by hand. Her business really was a labor of love.

"Or you can go grab something to eat with me," Colton said.

For a moment there was just silence.

He shrugged, unconcerned. "I'm starving. I need to eat."

"I am hungry," Jenny said, her stomach suddenly growling.

"That settled that," he answered. "We'll go eat."

Chapter Six

COLTON DROVE HER to Rocco's for dinner. Normally there was a wait at the popular Italian restaurant but the pretty hostess remembered Colton, and fell all over herself trying to get him a table right away, seating them in one of the big dark red leather booths against the wall.

Colton waited for Jenny to sit, and then slid into the booth seat opposite hers.

"I've never been here," she confessed, gazing around the restaurant. "It's quite charming."

Faux grapes dangled in red and purple clusters from the arbor trellis-covered ceiling. Murals of the golden and green Tuscan countryside adorned the walls. Red candles burned and dripped in straw-wrapped Chianti bottles on every red checked table cloth. A wall fountain tinkled with water and sound.

"It was quite the date place when I was in school," he answered. "I'm surprised no one ever brought you here."

She held her menu tight to her chest, as if it were a shield and she needed protection. And maybe she did because Colton was far too rugged and handsome in the candlelight.

"I didn't date a lot in high school."

"Why not?"

"I was shy. And painfully introverted. As well as a very late bloomer."

"I bet all those guys are kicking themselves now."

She flushed. "I doubt that." She opened her menu to hide her pink cheeks. "So what's good here? What would you recommend?"

"All the pasta dishes are homemade. I recommend them all, unless you're one of those women who won't eat carbs."

Jenny smiled. "I definitely eat carbs. I love pizza, and pasta and garlic bread and garlic cheese bread… the more cheese the better."

"Can't believe that. You're tiny."

"I run, and work out, but I also like to eat." Her gaze dropped back down to her menu, shy again. "I know you just got home. I feel bad taking you away from your family."

"Don't. We were just eating takeout tonight," he said, ignoring his menu. "And when I come home, I like to visit my favorite places, and Rocco's is one of my personal favorites. Came here with two other couples for my senior prom."

"I bet it was fun."

He nodded. "Where did you go?"

She reached for her water glass, took a quick sip. "I didn't go to the prom."

"I can't believe you weren't asked."

She sighed. "I was."

He waited.

She shrugged. "It wasn't… realistic. To go." She shrugged again. "So I didn't."

"Why wasn't it?"

"I didn't have the money for a dress and boutonniere and hair and all that stuff. And it wasn't a big deal, either," Jenny added quickly, before he could say something that would make her feel even more awkward. "He was a nice guy but we weren't dating, and it just was too much money for something that wasn't all that special."

"You don't think your senior prom is special?"

"I don't think being frivolous with money is smart." She looked up, their gazes colliding and holding. "I am actually quite cautious, and frugal." Her lips pursed and she made a soft rough mocking sound. "Not that you'd know it today. That wedding cost a fortune."

"Are your parents upset with you?"

She hesitated a little longer this time. "No. I'm lucky that way. They've never pushed me. Never had high expectations for me." Her lips curved wistfully. "I'm the one that puts pressure on me. I can be really hard on myself. I'm far too driven for my own good."

"Ambition isn't a bad thing."

"Not if you're Colton Thorpe and a national champion. But if you're just a secretary…" She shook her head, struggled to smile. "I hated being a secretary. But apparently I was good at it. Men loved my efficiency. My commitment. My ability to sacrifice my personal life for their professional life."

"You did that?"

"Daily. It was the job."

"Why would you?"

"Because eventually you get paid good money for being a valuable asset." Her smile turned mocking. "There are even bonuses when you become invaluable. So that's what I was determined to become, Charles Monmouth's invaluable executive assistant."

"I gather from what he was saying at Grey's, you succeeded."

"Yes."

"He wants you to return to Chicago with him," Colton added.

"But I won't. Even if I return to Chicago, I'd never work for him again. That part of my life is over." Her eyes suddenly stung and her chest ached again, a lump filling her throat making it hard to swallow. "Sorry," she said huskily, blinking to dry the tears. "I don't want to cry again. I can't stand crying. Makes me hate myself when I do it."

"You hate yourself for crying?"

She nodded. "Crying doesn't solve problems. And it's a sign of weakness. It's one of my rules of conduct—"

"You have rules of conduct?" he interrupted, creases fanning from his eyes, his deep voice tinged with laughter.

"Of course. Doesn't everyone?"

"Oh, probably a few. But it sounds funny for a pretty little girl like you to say she does."

Jenny ignored the pretty little girl part. "What are your rules?"

He leaned back against the booth, lips twitching, blue eyes warm. "Don't drink and drive. Don't hook up with married chicks. And don't piss off cops or any other law enforcement official. Jail's not fun."

She laughed. "You've been to jail?"

"Couple times."

"For what? Drinking, driving too fast, fighting?"

"Pretty much. But it's been ten years since I last got in trouble like that."

"What happened?"

"I got booked in Shreveport for public intoxication. Jail sobered me up real quick. Haven't been stupid that way since."

"You're not a big drinker?"

"I like a couple of beers. I don't like losing control."

That part certainly resonated with her. "I don't either. Which is why I hate crying."

His smile was easy. "I'm okay with women crying, but not a fan of a man crying, not unless his dog has died, and then I expect some tears."

Jenny laughed.

His eyes glimmered warm. "You have a pretty laugh. You should laugh more."

They stopped talking long enough to order dinner, and then kept conversation light while they shared bruschetta and a Caprese salad before their entrees arrived.

They each had a glass of red wine with dinner, just one, but the wine seemed to go straight to Jenny's head despite her plate of pumpkin raviolis in the most delicious sage and brown butter sauce she'd ever had.

Colton was right. The food was delicious here and she'd eaten a lot, but even with a full belly, she felt light-headed and breathless.

She was just too aware of Colton.

Too aware of the way the candlelight accented his high hard cheekbone and the little scar curving across the bone.

Too aware of his firm mouth and the press of his lips.

Too aware of the bronze of his skin at his throat and the taut planes of his chest beneath the thin knit t-shirt.

She'd never cared about Charles' appearance. She'd told herself she liked slender men, intellectual men. She'd convinced herself that looks didn't matter.

But suddenly she couldn't stop focusing on Colton's face and body and the way he moved, and the curl of his strong fingers as they held his fork, or reached for his wine glass.

Everything he did looked strong and smooth and beautiful.

Jenny swallowed hard and knotted her napkin in her lap, thinking if she didn't get home soon she'd get herself into some serious trouble. "That was lovely," she said. "And when the bill comes, I'll figure out my part. I think it's around forty dollars or so."

Colton's head lifted and he gave her a strange look. "Your part?"

"Yes. My half of the bruschetta and salad, the ravioli and the wine."

"I asked you to dinner."

"I know but it's not a date and I'm not going to let you pay—"

"I asked you to dinner," he repeated quietly.

"Yes, but—"

"This was my treat."

"You don't need to treat me."

"Are you trying to insult me?"

"No." She went hot, then cold. Her brow creased. "No. Not at all. I was simply trying to be fair."

"Fair," he repeated thoughtfully, studying her from across the table. "Speaking of fair, I'm going to ask you something and it might ruin what's been a very nice dinner, but I need to ask. So I can be fair to you. But did you love Charles? Deeply love him?"

An icy wave swept through her, suddenly sick, stomach churning. "I… loved… him. But I'm not sure what you mean by deeply love."

"Did you ever feel like you'd die without him?"

Jenny held her breath a moment, as the queasiness increased. She needed a moment to settle her nerves. "I loved that he was intelligent and ambitious. I loved that he was a risk-taker. I understood it. I thought I could be a good wife for him."

"Forgive me darlin', but that doesn't sound very romantic."

"I'm not—" she sucked her lip in, chewed it for courage, "—romantic. Never have been. Don't think I ever will be."

He gave her a long look.

Heart pounding, she forced a casual shrug. "Romance is overrated, Colton."

He gave her an even longer look, his expression revealing disbelief.

She felt as if she'd swallowed a bucket of nails. Her stomach hurt. Everything inside her hurt. Even her eyes felt gritty and dry, stinging from all the emotion she was suppressing, emotion that no one else would understand.

Colton would never understand what it'd been like.... the way people had looked at her, and her sisters. The pity. The sympathy. The judgment. The little girls were always dressed in clothes purchased at the thrift store on Front Street and they'd wear them until gray and threadbare. They'd wear their jackets until they were too tight on their shoulders and their wrists jutted out pale and knobby, little skeleton arms poking out of puffy winter coats. Coats were expensive. You didn't get a new one because you wanted a new one. You got a new one when there was absolutely nothing else you could wear.

She was marrying Charles because he was smart and successful and showed up for work, clean and sober. She admired his work ethic. She respected his ethic. His ethic resonated with her. She had the same drive. Becoming his partner had made sense to her. They could work together to accomplish shared goals. They wouldn't just survive. They'd flourish, and thrive.

By marrying Charles she could give her children everything she'd never had… parents who shared the same work ethic, parents who complimented each other's skills, parents who knew how to provide.

It hadn't seemed mercenary. It'd been practical. And practical was important. It was the thing missing in her childhood. There had been love, but there hadn't been enough of essentials like bread and milk, beef, chicken, and fresh vegetables.

"Marrying Charles meant that I could be a different woman than my mom," she said quietly, ending the uneasy silence. "It meant that my children would have a different life than I did. And that was—and still is—important to me. It would kill me if I had children and they had to go through what I went through. It was hard. Really hard."

"And yet it made you who you are today."

"Yes. Practical. Pragmatic. Unromantic." She struggled to smile but failed. "I know how it sounds. I've heard people whisper… she's just marrying Charles Monmouth for his money… but those people don't know him, or me. They don't know that I work twelve, thirteen hour days to make sure he succeeds. I wasn't marrying him to be on Easy Street. I was marrying him to be his partner. To help protect his career, and grow his business, and take it to the next level. I liked being instrumental to his success. I was an essential part of his team. It felt good to be needed, and rewarded. It felt good to finally be someone."

"You've always been someone."

"But it wasn't until I worked for Charles's company that I could do something for my family. My parents would have lost their house four years ago if I hadn't taken on their mortgage. My sisters were able to go to college because I took care of their tuition and books. And I didn't mind doing it. I was glad to do it. I was glad I could help. It made me proud."

"I don't disagree with anything you're saying. But who is taking care of you, Jenny?"

She lifted her chin. "I take care of myself."

"And what about love? True love? Mad, passionate love? You don't want that, either?"

She closed her eyes a moment, overwhelmed by pain. He was touching on old wounds and scars, pressing on bruises that suddenly were tender all over again. "I don't believe in it," she said faintly. "I don't believe that kind of love exists."

"Because you don't want to feel it?"

"Because I've never felt it."

"Not for anyone? Ever?"

He was staring hard at her, searching her face, and their eyes met, held, holding for so long that spots danced before her eyes.

Breathe, she told herself. *Breathe.*

She exhaled hard, eyes burning, stinging, heart aching.

She'd always had a crush on him, but it'd been immature and sweet, adolescent dreams fueled by a feverish imagination that had no relationship to reality.

She'd liked the teenage Colton—the tall, lanky boy body, his dark blonde hair, the blue eyes, the broad shoulders, his endless cocky confidence.

She still liked his hair, his face, his impressive male body with all the muscles and taut hard planes.

But there was more.

She wanted more.

She wanted to feel the weight of his hard muscular body, wanted the feel of his hands on her skin, his fingers against her breasts, his hips bearing down on hers.

She'd never craved sex before but she craved it now. Craved him, craving the things she'd never felt but believed he could make her feel. Pleasure. Satisfaction.

Maybe even peace.

Or maybe not.

But she was almost thirty and she'd been a hard worker and a dutiful daughter and an exceptional employee.

Now she wanted to feel like a woman. She wanted to feel as if she mattered, and her body mattered, and she wanted him to be the one to seduce her, satiate her.

He, with his big hard body and piercing blue eyes and deep raspy voice.

She wanted his hands and his mouth exploring her, his hard body filling her.

She wanted him. She wanted to be taken and pleasured.

Taken and satiated.

Taken.

Known.

COLTON FELT THE moment the energy changed between them, the air suddenly electric, charged with interest, crackling with awareness. Desire.

The desire wasn't one-sided. He'd wanted Jenny Wright from the moment he spotted her on the street corner in her fancy wedding gown.

But the desire now was sharper, harder, heavier.

His body felt heavy and hungry. He felt fierce, almost predatory and knew he wasn't what Jenny needed, particularly not hours after being jilted.

She needed a kind man, a gentle man, a man who would spoil her and treat her like a princess.

Colton didn't know how to do that.

His expertise was in the bedroom, and yeah, he had solid technique, but he knew Jenny didn't need a mind-blowing orgasm as much as she needed TLC.

Colt didn't have a clue how to give TLC.

"I should get you home," he said, fishing into his pocket for a wad of bills and peeling off four twenties and tucking them into the leather billfold.

She nodded and got to her feet. She rubbed her hands against the front of her thighs, as though she were nervous. Or excited. Probably both.

It would be so easy to kiss her right now. To slide his hands into her hair and wrap the silken strands around his fingers and hold her head back so he could take her mouth, exploring the softness and warmth as he molded her slim body to his.

He hardened all over again. He'd been in a state of arousal all night. It was ridiculous, being hard for hours, his aching erection straining against the denim.

They left Rocco's in silence. As they approach his truck, Jenny misjudged the curb and would have fallen if he hadn't reached for her, and held her up.

"Thanks for the save," she said, her voice pitched low. "Now I feel like Charles."

"You're not drunk," he answered, putting his arm around her to steady her. "You're just tired."

"I am," she agreed.

Colton kept his arm around her as he walked her to his truck. He could feel her warmth with her slender body tucked up against his side, and smell the scent of her shampoo. Her hair smelled good, she smelled good, and felt good.

He was sure she would taste just as good, too.

Just like that he went hot and hard all over again, and the heat surging through him tested his temper, testing his control.

He shouldn't want her this much. He shouldn't want anybody this much.

He was glad when they reached his truck. He opened the passenger door for her and stepped back to let her climb in.

But she didn't climb in. She turned around, faced him.

They were standing so close he could feel her breath and see the rise and fall of her breasts beneath her thin black sweater.

"I wish you were still a bad boy," she said quietly, her face tilted up to his, her wide brown eyes meeting his and holding.

"Why?" he asked, his fingers itching to push her long blonde hair back from her face so he could caress the sweep of her high cheekbone, and the beautiful line of her jaw.

"Because then you could make me forget today."

Colton swallowed hard, and counted to five before trusting himself to speak. "I'm not even going to go there, darlin'. It's bad enough you'll wake up with a headache. You don't need to wake up with a bunch of regrets."

"My only regret is that I've never had what I always wanted to have." Her lips curved but the smile didn't reach her eyes. "You."

"You don't want me, babe."

She reached out and placed a light hand on his chest, her fingers shaking. Her voice shook, too. "I've wanted you my whole life."

He didn't remember moving. He didn't mean to move toward her. He certainly didn't intend to kiss her. But suddenly his head dipped, blocking the moon, and his lips covered hers.

She shuddered as the touch of his mouth and something wild and fierce swept through him, and he drew her against him, close, so close, that he could feel the soft crush of her breasts against his chest and her tremulous breath as she inhaled.

"Easy," he murmured as her breath hitched, and then unable to help himself, he wrapped an arm around her, his hand low on her hips, his palm cupping her butt, urging her even closer because he couldn't remember the last time a woman felt this right in his arms, or a kiss made him feel this good.

When he finally let her go a few minutes later, they were both breathing hard and Jenny's brown eyes were huge, and her lips were soft, and almost bruised.

"Wow," she whispered, blinking at him, expression dazed.

He swallowed hard. God help him, but he felt the exact same way.

"I better get you home," he said gruffly, aware that if he didn't take her home now, she wouldn't be going home tonight. He'd be taking her somewhere private, somewhere that had a big bed and a door that locked, and a Do Not Disturb sign for the door.

She nodded once and silently climbed up into his truck.

Colton walked slowly around to the driver's seat. He had to walk slow. He needed the time to get his control back.

Chapter Seven

JENNY TOSSED AND turned in the twin bunk bed in her childhood bedroom.

She couldn't sleep. It was impossible to sleep when she felt so hot and bothered.

She wasn't used to feeling this way. She didn't get hot and bothered. At least, she'd never lost her head with Charles before.

Charles.

She shuddered, and drew the covers up to her chin, remembering how he'd barged into Grey's earlier in the night, as drunk as a skunk, insisting she come back to Chicago with him. Even though he didn't want to marry her.

She shuddered again, remembering how he kept grabbing at her, slurring as he talked.

And then Colton appeared and before she knew it, they were having dinner and talking and she was revealing far too much.

Colton made her feel far too much.

Funny how Charles made her feel cool and calm and beautifully composed. But Colton had the opposite effect. Colton stirred her up, made her restless, made her want things. Different things than she'd ever wanted before and the emotions weren't pleasant. The emotions scared her.

She turned over again, onto her stomach, clutching her pillow with both arms, humming with awareness. She could still feel Colton's mouth on hers, still feel the press of his hard body and it made her body tingle. She felt tense and yet alive, her emotions wild, her desires even wilder.

It was all she could do to stop thinking. It was another hour before she finally fell asleep.

JENNY WOKE UP to sunlight pouring through cracks in the blinds at her window. She glanced at the clock. Eight twenty. That was late for her to still be in bed.

Leaving her room, she spotted her parents in the living room, watching the morning news. They were both engrossed in the broadcast and she continued on to the kitchen where she filled a mug with what was left of the coffee.

Jenny drank her coffee black. She had never liked it black, but Charles told her his best assistants drank only black coffee. It had no calories and was faster to make, with less wasted time stirring in creamers and sweeteners.

Charles.

She shook her head, wondering what had possessed her to turn herself inside out to please him. To be perfect for him. Which meant becoming no one… just a pretty, accommodating shell of a woman.

What an idiot.

Not just him, but her. She was the one who'd wanted—imagined—that becoming nothing would earn his respect.

She stared down into her black coffee, the color like thin tar.

She hated black coffee. It was bitter and nasty and she liked it rich and sweet. She liked flavor and color. Liked things to taste good and feel good—

Jenny wrenched open the refrigerator door, took the milk from the door, and poured a generous measure into her cup, topping off her coffee. She dumped in a big spoonfull of sugar and then smiled as she stirred, vigorously stirring, swirling the spoon around and around, listening to the metal clink against the ceramic mug, enjoying the scraping sound of the spoon at the bottom of the cup.

She was going to live this week.

She was going to savor every moment, suck every ounce of pleasure from her time home before she returned to Chicago, and she hoped that part of the pleasure was seeing Colton again.

No, he wasn't safe. Just thinking about him made her pulse quicken and adrenaline race through her.

He was handsome and tough, and overwhelmingly physical. She didn't feel calm around him. She felt wild.

They had no future together but she didn't need the future. She needed now.

She needed to live now.

Jenny was taking her first sip of coffee when her mom entered the kitchen.

"This was on the doorstep this morning," her mother said, giving her the envelope with *Jenny* written on the front.

Jenny didn't recognize the handwriting and tore it open.

Inside was one of her diamond and pearl drop earrings and a note.

I found the earring on the seat this morning, knew you'd be worried and wanted to get it back to you.

I'm going to Brock Sheenan's ranch this morning to look at one of his bulls. Call me if you feel like going. Should be a pretty drive. I'm heading out around nine.
Colt

He'd also scrawled his phone number.

Jenny looked up to find her mother watching her. She held up the earring. "Colton Thorpe found my earring."

"He brought you home last night, didn't he?" her mother asked, no expression in her voice, or on her face.

Jenny nodded. "We bumped into him at Grey's Saloon. And then went to Rocco's for dinner."

"You and the girls? Or you and the girls, and Colton? Or…?"

"Just Colton and me." Jenny saw the flicker of emotion in her mother's eyes that time. "You still don't like him, do you?"

Her mother took a second to answer and then chose her

words with care. "He earned his reputation for a reason."

"That was fourteen years ago."

"From what I hear, he hasn't changed much. He's not interested in responsibility, or commitments."

"Apparently Charles wasn't either," Jenny muttered under her breath.

"Mandy and Charity are friendly with his sister, Tricia. Colton doesn't come home often, and yes, he'll send money home, but he's left his mother's care to his sister, and that's not right. A man takes care of his family. Remember that."

It was on the tip of Jenny's tongue to make a comment about her father, but that would be unkind, and would only create tension so she swallowed the remark and nodded, even as she resented her own values and ethics that had made her so cautious in life. So controlling over her situation.

Jenny suddenly wanted to be that girl who was free. She wanted to have a wild streak, an impulsive streak, one that allowed her to take risks and be adventurous, and take the path never traveled.

Her path was so familiar, so very well-traveled that it bored her.

"Jenny, I know you're hurt, and hurting," her mother added, her brow still creased, concern in her dark eyes. "I know you're searching for answers right now, too, but Colton Thorpe isn't the right answer. And how do I know that? Because your father was like Colton Thorpe. He was handsome and popular and wildly exciting and I threw everything away to be with him. Do I love your father? Yes. But our lives have not been easy, and there have been regrets. I'm sure you know I've had regrets. So just be smart. Think with your head, not your heart, and whatever you do, don't sleep with him. Don't let yourself get that close to him. Men like Colton and your father are great in bed, but they're not men that make good life partners."

Jenny had never heard her mother speak so candidly about life or marriage, much less her own difficult marriage, and her mother's words had weight, and made a significant impression.

Jenny gave her mother a hug and headed outside to the front porch with her coffee.

Chance Avenue was relatively quiet this morning. Leaves fell from trees. A dog barked once, twice behind a fence as a little boy shot a basketball through a portable hoop in his driveway.

She glanced down the street, saw the rows of small houses and cars, but she could see no rusty orange red truck.

She looked at her watch. Five of nine. It looked like Colton had already left for Brock Sheenan's ranch.

Her chest ached a little. She straightened her shoulders. She pretended she felt nothing. It was good that he'd gone. She shouldn't go. Couldn't go. Not after everything her mother had said.

COLTON'S PHONE RANG at five minutes to nine. He was at the gas station down the street from the hardware store filling his truck when the phone rang, and as he dug the phone from his back pocket, he thought maybe it was Jenny calling.

It wasn't. It was his mom.

She hoped he hadn't left for Paradise Valley yet. She'd run out of her favorite pain reliever and hoped he could pick some up at the store.

"I'm at the gas station right now, and they have a little mini market," he told her. "As soon as I'm done, I'll go buy you some and will be home in a few minutes."

Off the phone, Colton finished filling the tank and gazed at the steep mountain slopes framing Marietta. Copper Mountain, one of the largest peaks in the Gallatin Range was to the west, with the Absaroka Range to the east. He loved these two ranges, had grown up in their shadow, and he looked forward to this morning's drive to Brock's ranch. Fall was beautiful in Montana and the colors were so striking now with their leaves all shades of russet and gold.

The pump clicked off and he replaced the nozzle, screwed the cap on the tank and headed inside to pay. He picked up the pain killer for his mom, feeling guilty that although he was home, he wasn't spending more time with her.

He loved his mother. She'd been a wonderful mother but she wasn't the same since his father died. His dad had always helped her manage her diabetes, but now that he was gone, Mom wouldn't help herself. She didn't like testing her blood glucose. She didn't like pricking her finger. She didn't like her insulin injections. She didn't like eating properly. She didn't like having diabetes and said she was done trying, done taking care of herself.

Colton didn't know how to respond to that.

He didn't know what to say or do. He'd tried giving pep talks and encouraging her to get out and meet people. He'd arranged for a special senior shuttle to come by and pick her up and take her places. The shuttle had a lift for her wheelchair and they could make sure she had mobility, but his mom wouldn't go. His mom wouldn't leave the house unless he or Tricia took her somewhere, and Colton couldn't live like that.

He wouldn't be chained to helplessness.

He didn't believe in controlling someone through guilt and he resented being manipulated.

So he stopped coming home and he still sent money but it wasn't the same, he knew it wasn't.

As a son, he should be doing more for her. He should be staying in touch better. He should maybe even live here, and have her move in with him.

He knew it.

But he couldn't do it. He couldn't move back here, and he couldn't fly in every weekend to give Tricia a break. He'd pay for a nurse or attendant, but he wouldn't become the attendant.

There were still so many things he wanted in life, so many things he wanted to do and be.

And so when he did come home, like he was now, he was conflicted. Home wasn't a simple thing. Coming home always made him feel guilty.

JENNY WAS STILL on the porch with her coffee when Colton drove past in his loud Chevy truck. He spotted her on the porch and then braked, then put his truck into reverse and backed up a few feet until he was in front of her house.

"'Morning," he said.

"Hi."

"Nice pajamas," he said, smiling.

She glanced down at her gray striped leggings and long light blue Sleeping Beauty nightshirt and then smiled up at him. "These are classics found in my bedroom dresser's bottom drawer." She couldn't stop smiling. She was glad to see him. She'd wanted to see him, and Colton had such warm blue eyes, and his teeth looked so white this morning against his golden tan. "Thank you for finding my earring."

"I thought about keeping it, but it might have been a bit feminine for me."

She laughed out loud. "You're ridiculous."

"I am." He hesitated. "Most definitely."

For a moment they just looked at each other and Jenny's

chest grew tight as the silence stretched.

She wanted to say something. Wanted to tell him something that would keep him here, talking to her, but she had nothing to say. They really had nothing to say to each other. There was no reason for them to talk, or be together.

Colton seemed to come to the same conclusion. "I better go," he said after a moment. "I need to drop something off at my mom's and then get on the road. I promised Brock I'd be there before ten."

She nodded. "Okay."

He nodded.

Her chest ached with bottled air.

"All right." He gave her a faint, crooked smile and lifted a hand in farewell.

Jenny's eyes burned as he pulled away from the curb.

Let him go. Let him go.

She couldn't let him go.

"Colton!" She called, moving down the porch steps to the cracked concrete sidewalk.

He braked, stuck his head out the window, looked back at her. "Yes, princess?"

Her heart was hammering so hard it felt as if it'd burst. This was stupid. So stupid. She shouldn't—

"Can I go with you?" she called to him, her voice too high and thin. But she was nervous. So nervous. "To Brock's place?" She gulped a breath for courage. "It's going to be a beautiful day. I'd love to go for the drive. That is, if it's not too late."

Colton's firm mouth eased. His blue gaze warmed. "It's never too late. Go change and I'll be back in a few minutes to scoop you up. How much time do you need? Fifteen? Twenty?"

She shook her head, already climbing the steps. "Just five."

"Just five?"

She grinned. "We could say four."

He laughed, creases fanning from his eyes. "Big talker."

"Time me."

"Fine. The clock is ticking now."

HIS MOM NEEDED more than five minutes of his time, and Colton didn't make it back to his truck until nine-thirty.

Jenny was waiting on her front porch for him, dressed in skinny jeans, leather boots, and a fuzzy oversized caramel-colored sweater that hung half way down to her knees. She'd pulled her long blonde hair into a ponytail and looked like a high school cheerleader, young and fresh and very sweet.

He watched her climb into his truck, thinking it felt right to have her there on the bench seat next to him. It felt so right that it would be easy to lean over and kiss her, as if she was his girl.

He was ready to kiss her again. He wanted to feel her warmth and softness. Wanted to taste her mouth again. He'd liked kissing her. He'd wanted to keep kissing her last night. Had wanted to kiss all of her and discover her and make her his.

The last time he'd felt this way about a woman he'd married her.

And he knew how that turned out.

Chapter Eight

JENNY CURLED UP on the bench seat of the truck, enjoying the country music playing on the old truck's radio and the rugged beauty of the Montana landscape beyond her window painted in strokes of green, yellow, blue, and gold.

After leaving Highway 89, they'd taken one of the long narrow roads that cut away from the Yellowstone river to wind up through foothills and pastures, with cabins and ranch houses dotting the land on either side.

The jagged Absarokas already had a little snow dusting the higher peaks and it was predicted that more snow was coming in the next few weeks, but today was dry and fine, with temperatures expected to be in the high sixties to low seventies, not that it'd be that warm on Brock's ranch, which nestled in the valley tucked deep in the Absaroka Range.

"Do you know Brock?" Colton asked her as they continued to climb higher in the foothills and the valley spread below them, with the Yellowstone River sparkling like a dark blue ribbon against the gold and green fields.

"I don't know him, but I went to school with one of the Sheenans. Dillon, I think it was. The rest were all older.

They're a big family, aren't they?"

Colton nodded. "Five boys, one girl, but only Brock and Trey still live around here. The rest have moved East or West. Cormac and Troy have been very successful. It's Troy who financed that massive renovation on The Graff. Ten million went into that hotel. Crazy. I think it was a waste of money."

"The hotel is beautiful," Jenny protested. "It's back to its original splendor, and now it's been designated a historical landmark."

"I just wouldn't ever put that kind of money into a building, much less a building here in Marietta. Marietta is a dying town—"

"You think so?"

"Maybe not dying," he corrected. "But I wouldn't call it thriving."

"I totally disagree. I think Marietta looks terrific. I see new growth all over the place." Jenny felt ready to battle and she wasn't even sure why. Her childhood had been far from idyllic and yet she loved this town. She loved Crawford County, tucked between Gallatin and Park counties. It was an inspiring part of the country, blessed with an abundance of natural beauty. "And I didn't know that Troy Sheenan was behind the big renovation at The Graff, but I'm glad he did it. I'm glad he saved a historic property so that future generations can enjoy it."

Colton laughed softly. "You certainly got feisty, princess.

I had no idea you loved Marietta so much."

Jenny thought about it for a moment and then laughed, too. "Until just now, I didn't, either."

He shot her a side glance as his truck rattled across the cattle guard marking the entrance to Brock's Copper Mountain Ranch. "So when are you moving back to Marietta?"

When she didn't immediately reply, he asked, "You are moving back to Marietta, aren't you? Or are you going to return to Chicago?"

"All my things are in Chicago."

He gave her another searching look. "That doesn't mean you need to stay there. You can just as easily pack your things up and move home."

Jenny didn't know how to answer that, and Colton let the subject drop as Brock's two-story log cabin home came into view.

Big cedar and pine trees grew in clusters around the sprawling log-cabin style home, while a big gray barn sat back behind the house, flanked by several corrals. Two horses stopped grazing to come to the front of the corral to greet them as Colton parked next to the other trucks and trailers near the barn.

Colton gave each of the horses attention, rubbing noses, and giving pats. He glanced at Jenny, who had hung back.

"You don't like horses?" he asked.

"I don't dislike them. I just haven't been around them much."

"Fair enough." He gestured for her to follow him. "Brock should be in the back, with the bulls."

They tramped across gravel to dirt, and on into the barn, fragrant with hay, leather, dung, and warm animals.

Jenny's nose wrinkled. It was a peculiar smell. Not bad. But… different.

Colton struggled not to laugh. "Is this your first time in a barn?"

"No. In school we went on a field trip to a ranch. To Sage Carrigan's ranch. I think it's around here someplace."

"The Carrigans' ranch, Circle C, is further back in Paradise Valley. We passed the MacCreadies' place already, and the Douglases'. If we had kept going on the main road, we would have reached Brock's dad's place, and then the Circle C Ranch butts up against the Sheenans'."

"Why didn't Brock want to work his family's ranch?"

"Brock wanted to be his own boss, do his own thing, and here he can."

"You can't grow a lot of crops up this high, can you?"

"No. This is grazing land, ranching land, and it's not easy in winter. Brock's got his work cut out for him here."

A gray and white dog raced into the far end of the barn, barking wildly, and then another dog joined the first, barking too.

A big black-haired man followed the dogs into the barn and called a curt command. Both dogs instantly stopped barking and sat down, tongues hanging from their mouths.

"Colt," the man said, walking towards them hand outstretched. "Good to see you." He shook Colton's hand. "It's been a long time."

"Couple years at least," Colton agreed. He turned to Jenny and introduced her. "Brock, this is my friend Jenny Wright. We grew up together on Chance."

Jenny shook Brock's hand. He was tall and she had to tip her head back to see him. He had dark brown eyes that looked almost black in the barn's natural light. "Nice to meet you, Brock," she said.

After the handshake, Brock's hands went to his hips and he frowned as he tried to place her name. "How do you spell your last name?" he asked her. "W-r-i-g-h-t?"

Jenny nodded.

"I know your name. Why?" he asked.

"I went to school with Dillon. He was a couple years older, but we were both at Marietta High at the same time."

He shook his head. "That's not it." He kept studying her and then he snapped his fingers. "Your dad isn't Tom, is he?"

Jenny's eyes widened. She nodded.

"He worked at the high school," Brock said. "When I was there. Didn't he?"

Jenny's mouth had dried. She nodded once. Yes. Her dad had worked at the school. He'd been the janitor for four years before losing his job due to his problems with alcohol.

"I thought so," Brock said, smiling for the first time.

"Nice guy. Really nice guy. Is he still alive?"

Jenny nodded again.

"Good. Glad to hear it. Will you give him my best?"

Jenny felt a lump form in her throat. She was grateful for Brock's kindness. "I will."

After that the conversation turned to two of Brock's bulls, the younger bull the son of the older, and how Brock thought they might be good bucking bulls for the rodeo circuit, which is why he wanted Colton's perspective.

Jenny followed the men through to the outside paddock. The two bulls were in separate areas, but even then, they stood back from each other on either side of the fence in a faceoff.

They were huge animals, with big heads and horns and massive shoulders.

"You really ride those?" Jenny asked Colton, during a pause in Colton and Brock's discussion.

He smiled at her. "Crazy, huh?"

"Yes."

"My mom thinks so, too."

"Why do you do it then?"

"I like the rush. The money isn't bad. And I happen to be good at it."

She watched one of the big dark brown bulls paw the ground, and toss his head. "But it's dangerous."

Colton shrugged. "Life's dangerous. But you can't let that stop you."

After a bit, the three of them headed inside Brock's house to warm up with some hot coffee and fresh cinnamon bread made by his housekeeper, an older woman who silently came and went as they sat at the dining room table talking.

Except for Brock and his housekeeper, his big log cabin was quiet and no lights were on upstairs. The dining room, even with the lights on, had a vaguely empty air, as if it was seldom used. It certainly lacked decorative touches that could be called feminine touches, like curtains at the window, art on the wall, a centerpiece for the big oak table. No, it was very much a man's house, a bachelor house, just as Brock struck Jenny as a confirmed bachelor too.

She wasn't sure why she'd decided he was a bachelor. He was mid to late thirties and fit, with the taut, honed muscles of one who worked hard for a living. He had excellent manners, too, and could channel warmth when required, so she wondered if it was his grooming that made him appear a little unsettled, perhaps even a little less civilized, as he wore his thick black hair rather long and shaggy, and his jaw had so much black stubble it could pass as a beard. Thus it was a shock to Jenny when Colton asked about Brock's kids.

"How are the twins?" Colton asked.

"They're good. Getting big," Brock said, stirring restlessly in his chair. "Eleven now."

"Pre-teens," Jenny said.

Brock nodded. "They don't live here now, not during the school terms. They're both at a prep school on the East

Coast. It was hard to see them go, but they needed to be pushed, and they needed the structure. They were starting to get into trouble here, and lag academically, and I couldn't have that. I promised Amy they'd go to college. Do all the things she and I didn't do, so they're off in Connecticut now. But they should be home for Christmas." He rose abruptly, gestured to their empty coffee cups. "Would you like a refill?"

Colton shook his head and stood, too. "No. We should go. I've promised to take my mom shopping later today. I ought to get on the road."

Brock walked them to Colton's rusty orange red truck, and he stood in the gravel driveway, seeing them off, his two Australian shepherds flanking him as he watched the truck drive away.

It took them almost fifteen minutes of traveling the steep winding mountain lane to get back on the main road. Brock's Copper Mountain Ranch would definitely see snow sooner than low-lying ranches. Jenny couldn't imagine being trapped up there after one of the big storms. A heavy snow fall would keep you there for days, if not weeks.

"I liked him," Jenny said. "But he's different, isn't he? Strikes me as reclusive."

"He's always been a bit of a loner, but he's become even more isolated in the past few years. I'm not sure him sending the kids to boarding school was the best idea. The kids kept him connected to the world and active in the community. It was good for him. The kids were good for him," Colton answered.

"Where's their mom?"

"She died eleven years ago, was killed in a car accident just after the twins were born." Colton braked at the highway, gauging traffic before merging. "The accident took place just a quarter mile from here. A drunk driver took her out. Brock's raised the kids ever since."

"Now that you mention it, I think I remember hearing news about the accident. It happened right around the holidays. She was young, too."

Colton nodded. "They were both pretty young. They'd been high school sweethearts. Married right out of school. He worked the ranch but she'd make the drive into Marietta where she worked at the bank on Main Street. She was a teller. She hated leaving the babies to go work but they needed her paycheck." Colton fell silent. "It was terrible. The funeral. It was terrible for years after. Brock's not had an easy life, and those kids have needed a mother." He glanced at Jenny, a smile lurking in his eyes. "Apparently, things are looking up for him, though. I stay in touch with his brother Trey and Trey said Brock's dating. It might even be serious. We're all hoping it is. He deserves a good woman, and the twins need a loving mom."

Colton shot her another quick glance a few moments later. "You've gone all quiet."

"Just thinking about everything you said. Brock does

seem awfully alone."

"Then let's hope this new woman in his life is the right one and maybe soon we will have a wedding—" he broke off, grimacing. "Sorry. That's got to still sting."

She shrugged. "The shock's wearing off. Acceptance is setting in. Which is good," she added quickly. "I can see now that marrying Charles would have been a mistake. I think I had to come home to see it. In Chicago I could pretend to be someone else, but here in Marietta it's hard to escape facts. Hard not to see me for who I am, and to realize that I've spent years trying to change myself to win approval. I don't want to do that anymore."

He nodded approvingly. "Good. You shouldn't have to."

~

THEY STOPPED A few minutes later for a quick lunch at a little barbecue place in Emigrant Gulch on their way back to town.

The barbecue place wasn't much bigger than a double-wide trailer surrounded by gravel, but the smell of slow-roasted pork and beef wafting from the open front door made Jenny's mouth water. She hadn't thought she was hungry until now.

They sat down at one of the long picnic tables in the center of the room, and studied the menu. It all looked good to Jenny. "Order for me," she said, tossing the menu back onto the table.

He closed his menu, and leaned towards her, big arms braced on the table. "No preferences?"

"It all sounds good."

"Even the barbecued testicles?"

"What?" she cried, reaching for the menu to have a second look.

"Just kidding," he answered, closing his menu with a grin. "They don't have them. Here." His eyes gleamed at her. "Want anything else, darlin'?"

Her pulse jumped. Her insides did a wild flip.

Did she want anything else? Oh yes… yes she did.

She touched the tip of her tongue to her upper lip, her mouth suddenly very dry. "Like…?"

He stared into her eyes, searching them, letting her see the heat in his own. The heat made her melt and her mouth just grew drier. She sucked in her bottom lip, feeling parched.

He cocked an eyebrow, his expression wicked. "I could get you whatever you like."

For a moment she couldn't breathe, much less think. Her imagination went into overdrive, fueled by possibilities.

What would she like?

Everything…

He laughed softly and reached out to tap the tip of her nose. "Soda, iced tea, water. They might even have lemonade."

Oh. That's what he meant. A drink. Beverages. She nodded, blushing. "Yes. I'm super thirsty. Water would be great."

Still grinning, he got to his feet. "Water coming right up."

She watched him walk to the counter to place their lunch order. She knew she was staring at him as he walked, but it was impossible not to admire his neat hips, his long legs, and the way the denim wrapped his muscle, hugging it.

It was even more impossible to forget how he'd felt against her, last night. His body was hard and warm. Beautifully warm, incredibly, seductively solid.

That kiss, there, next to his truck, had blown her mind.

That kiss made her want to take risks, giant risks, and for the next few days at least, just live.

The girl working at the counter was eying Colton with open appreciation. She was a tall, slender redhead, a very pretty redhead, and when she said something to Colton that made him smile, Jenny felt a strange sharp pain in her chest. The pain grew worse when Colton answered the girl, and made her laugh.

Jenny closed her eyes, stunned by the stab of jealousy.

She'd never felt jealous before—

No, not true. She'd been jealous of every girlfriend Colton had ever had back when she was in junior high. It hadn't mattered that Colton didn't even know she existed. It still hurt to think of him out with girls, talking with them, flirting, making out in some parked car.

She wanted to be his girl.

And from the sharp pang she felt now as the redhead flirted with Colton, Jenny knew a part of her still wanted to be Colton's girl.

Silly Jenny. Always wanting what she couldn't have.

Colton returned to the table with two bottles of water. "Lunch will be just a few minutes," he said, twisting off the cap from one water bottle before handing it to her.

This time, he didn't sit on the opposite side of the table, he sat down next to her at the picnic table, facing out, his back resting against the table, his shoulder practically touching hers.

Jenny turned on the bench, too, to make it easier to see him. They'd sat close in the truck but this somehow felt different. "The girl behind the counter," Jenny said. "Did she know you?"

"No. Why?"

"She just seemed....really friendly."

"Oh, she was. Very friendly." He looked at her, expression shuttered. "Did that bother you?"

"No."

His eyebrow lifted.

"No." She frowned at her water. "No, it didn't bother me, but it seemed strange. She knows you're here with me but she was so flirty."

He shot her an amused glance. "Maybe she thought we were just friends."

"Well, we are just friends."

"Maybe she thought we were brother and sister," he added.

"Could be," Jenny muttered, hating him right then, as well as the sexy redhead behind the counter.

Colton's soft laugh was a rumble in his chest.

She'd lifted her chin in silent protest, when Colton suddenly leaned towards her, closing the distance to murmur. "Maybe we need to make sure we're not brother and sister..."

And then he covered her mouth with his, in a slow, warm searching kiss that quickly went from sweet and tentative to explosive heat.

Her mouth opened beneath the pressure of his lips, and she welcomed the stab of his tongue, his tongue stroking hers, teasing hers, stirring her senses and nerves so that she felt hot and molten, as if some of Sage's dark rich chocolate melted down to the warmest, sweetest liquid.

She felt liquid by the time Colton ended the kiss. Astonished she stared into his eyes after he lifted his head.

"You should warn a girl when you do something like that," she whispered, breathless. "Maybe call the fire department. Get a paramedic. 'Cause you are dangerous."

He laughed, a deep sexy laugh before kissing her lightly on the mouth, his breath and lips warm against hers, his skin smelling of soap and shaving cream and a hint of spice.

Her breath caught in her throat and she struggled to control her wildly beating heart.

Colton Thorpe was quickly turning her world inside out.

Chapter Nine

Lunch arrived—two beef brisket sandwiches—with potato salad and coleslaw, but Jenny couldn't see straight to eat.

She couldn't think clearly, either. Quite frankly, she couldn't think at all.

She stared at Colton, dazed, not just by the intensity of her emotions, but by the hot, fierce rush of lust. *Lust.* Jenny, who had found it shockingly easy to remain a virgin into her twenties, now felt positively wanton around Colton.

"Yes, princess?" he asked, a crooked smile curving his beautiful mouth, pushing aside his plate to focus on her.

"Did I say something?" she asked huskily.

He reached out to strum his thumb over her quivering lips. "No, but maybe you should, because it'd be so easy to haul you out to my truck and pull you down onto my lap and kiss you the way I want to kiss you."

She blinked, very much liking the sound of it. "Okay."

He laughed quietly, his blue eyes sparking at her. "Okay." Laughing again, he reached for his sandwich, but his gaze continued to rest on her.

It wasn't until they were driving home that Jenny found the nerve to ask him about his love life. "Are you a romantic, Colton?"

She'd caught him off guard and he turned his head and gave her a sharp look. "What?"

"You asked me yesterday if I'd ever been madly, passionately in love, and I was wondering, have you?"

He turned his gaze back to the road but his brow was furrowed and he didn't look happy about her question. "I believe in love, yeah."

But Jenny wasn't satisfied with his answer. She wanted more than that and she tugged on her sleeve, pulling the soft fuzzy knit down over her wrist, hiding her hand. "So you've felt like you'd die without someone? That losing her would break your heart?"

Colton drummed his fingers against the steering wheel. "Yeah."

Jenny glanced at him. "So you don't think romantic love is an illusion?"

COLTON SIGHED INWARDLY, and shifted on the seat, and then drummed his fingers again, hating the turn their conversation had taken. He did not want to talk about his love life, or his past, not with Jenny, not with anyone. "No," he said brusquely.

Her head lifted and she looked at him with those wide

brown eyes of hers, her gaze searching. But from her expression Jenny wasn't ready to drop the subject. "Was it as wonderful as they say?" she asked.

He stifled another sigh, telling himself he owed Jenny something. He'd certainly asked a lot of questions of her last night at dinner. "Falling in love is great," he said shortly. "Falling out of love…not so great. In fact, it's pretty damn awful."

"Did you want to marry her?"

He laughed once, low and rough. "I *did* marry her."

Jenny's brown grew huge. "But you're not married anymore?"

"No. Divorced a couple years ago."

"How long were you married?"

Colton tensed, abs tightening. "Long enough to know I'll never get married again."

She visibly winced. "That bad?"

"There were parts that were good. I like the idea of marriage, and I think it works for some people, but I've no desire to repeat the experience. I'm happy to be with a woman, and I enjoy female company, but I'm not about to become her meal ticket."

She stiffened and leaned back against the seat, averting her face to look out the window. They were approaching north Marietta. The gas station near The Wolf Den was coming up. They'd be passing Park Elementary soon and then would be on Chance Avenue in no time.

"That's harsh," she murmured, after a moment.

He shrugged, irritated, and not sure if it was more annoyed with her or himself. "But true."

"Marriage was that bad?"

"*My* marriage was that bad."

"I'm sorry."

He shrugged. "It was a good life lesson. One I needed to learn. And one I'll never forget."

They finished the drive in silence, and he told himself he was glad for the quiet. Better to have silence than discuss something that would just create friction and tension.

They were still in an uneasy silence when he pulled up in front of her house. He parked the truck, and came around the side to open her door for her. "I enjoyed today," he said, giving her his hand to help her out.

She looked at his hand, and then up into his face, before carefully getting out of the truck without accepting his help. "I did, too." She stepped onto the scraggly patch of grass tucked between the curb and sidewalk. "Thank you."

She was saying all the right things, he thought, but her tone was injured, as if he'd been the one to stir things up and turn a wonderful day upside down.

"Any time," he said tersely.

She lifted her eyebrows. "Don't say things you don't mean, cowboy."

"What do you mean?"

"I can tell you're upset with me. You didn't like that I

asked you questions, but last night you sure skewered me. But I get it. It's a man's world. You guys have your double standards."

"*What?*"

"Don't play dumb. You know exactly what I'm talking about, Colton Thorpe."

And then with a cool, dismissive nod in his direction she turned around and marched off to her house, head high, shoulders straight, looking like a high stepping drum major leading the band in the town parade.

And damn, but he wanted her.

He wanted her naked and straddling his hips. He wanted her on her back and open to him. He wanted her on all fours—

He just plain wanted Jenny.

So Colton, who didn't chase anybody, chased after her, following her up the steps to her sagging porch and stopping her at the front door.

"I'm sorry," he said, grabbing her arm and turning her around so she'd face him. "I'm sorry I haven't been more forthcoming about my marriage but it hurt. It sucked. I loved my wife but she didn't love me and maybe it's a male thing, but it *is* tough to talk about something that I didn't understand and will never understand but that's just life. She wanted me. She didn't want me. She wanted someone else. She got out. Okay?"

Jenny nodded once, a small nod, but he could see how

her brown eyes had darkened and filmed with tears. “Okay,” she whispered.

“Shit,” he swore. “I didn’t mean to make you cry.”

“I’m not crying,” she said, even as she reached up to run a knuckle beneath each eye, making sure both eyes were dry.

His hands settled on her shoulders, then slid down to her arms. She felt warm and small and tender and he was kicking himself for being an ass. “I hate that I hurt you. I like you, Jenny.” His voice dropped, his hands slid back up to her shoulders, and then in to her collarbones, and slowly up her neck to frame her beautiful face. “I like being around you,” he added, his voice deepening. “And I definitely like kissing you. But if we’re not careful, pretty soon it’s going to be a lot more than kissing.” He dipped his head, kissed her soft mouth, thinking he could kiss her all day. “Damn girl,” he said gruffly, lifting his head to look down into her eyes, “you’re hard on my self-control.”

She stared up at him. “Maybe you don’t need so much self-control.”

“But I do. Around you I do.”

“Why?”

“Because you don’t know me, darlin’. I’m not the kind of guy you fall for.”

He saw her lips part, heard her soft hiss of air.

“Maybe it’s you, Colton Thorpe, that doesn’t know the first thing about me.”

“What does that mean?” he asked. “And are you crying?”

"*No.*" She broke free, and took a step back, bumping into the front door. "I'm not crying, but yes, I am frustrated. You frustrate me. You always have."

"Why?"

"Because you're… *you.* Colton Thorpe." Her smile came and went. "My crush."

He frowned, confused.

She lifted her shoulders in a small, helpless shrug. "Growing up, I idolized you. Had the worst crush on you. The crush lasted for years, too."

"I left town at eighteen. You couldn't have been more than fourteen."

"Fourteen and about to start high school."

"And you liked me?"

"*Adored* you." Her lips quivered. "Thought you were the most amazing man ever." She let out a gurgle of embarrassed laughter. "Even with your horrible reputation. You were such a bad boy. My parents used to talk about you late at night. They'd warn us girls to stay away from you. You were trouble."

"Trouble," he repeated.

"Hell on wheels, my dad used to say." For a moment there was just silence and then she looked at him, a furrow in her brow. "Are you still trouble, Colton Thorpe?"

He didn't answer for the longest time. And then the corner of his mouth lifted in a small hard smile, a smile that was more bitter than sweet. "Yeah, Princess. I am. I guess that's what I've been trying to say. I'm no good. At least, not for a nice girl like you."

COLTON'S WORDS PLAYED over and over in Jenny's head after he'd climbed back into his truck and driven on home.

He wasn't good for a nice girl like her.

But maybe they all had it wrong. Maybe she wasn't a nice girl. Maybe she'd never been a nice girl.

She certainly hadn't been nice when she'd settled for a marriage that was loveless, passionless.

The question teased her the rest of the afternoon. The question continued to torment her that evening.

She loved every moment she spent with Colton. Loved how he made her feel. Loved the crazy adrenaline in her veins. It was so novel, so exciting. She was humming with emotion and need.

Suddenly she was awake. Aware. Suddenly she felt hungry, wild, fierce.

Life was full of so many possibilities. Anything could happen. Everything could happen. And she wanted everything to happen.

The rational part of her brain knew how this would go. Colton would leave after the rodeo ended and she'd return to Chicago, and she'd look for another job, and become the responsible, orderly executive assistant she used to be. She'd once again suppress her own needs and desires, because dedicated assistants didn't have needs and desires. No, dedicated assistants had just one goal—and that was to serve. To please.

But she wasn't in Chicago yet. She was still unemployed, and therefore, free. She could do what she wanted, which meant, try all the things she'd ever tried before. She could be wild now, even wanton.

She could want something for herself. Like pleasure.

She could want touch and sensation and sex. Amazing sex. Shouldn't a girl have amazing sex once in her life?

Sex would be amazing with Colton. She knew it. She could feel it. Just being around him made her ache. Just being near him made her warm, wet.

Colton was wrong.

She wasn't a nice girl. She didn't want to be treated like a nice girl, either. She wanted to be the girl who slept with bad boy Colton Thorpe.

She wanted hot sex, dirty sex, wanted the experience of being with him. Taken by him. However it would be.

But he's not safe, a little part of her whispered as she turned out the lights, and climbed into bed.

And maybe that's good, another part of her whispered, as she rolled onto her back to stare up at the dark bedroom ceiling.

Maybe that's what she needed. Someone like Colton to make her feel. Someone like Colton who was real and physical and carnal and sexual. But no. Not just someone *like* Colton, Colton Thorpe himself.

She was still awake an hour later. It was nearly midnight but sleep was elusive and she grabbed her phone and impulsively texted him. *What if I'm not a nice girl?* she typed, hitting SEND before she could change her mind.

Her stomach hurt as she waited for a reply. She prayed he'd reply. And soon.

He did, almost right away.

You don't want to go there, Princess.

Jenny studied his answer, then replied. *Maybe I do.*

He texted back right away. *Have you been drinking?*

No, she answered, *I'm in bed. And completely sober. My parents don't allow alcohol in the house anymore.*

Hell, darlin', I couldn't focus on anything after the I'm in bed part.

She smiled, blushed, chewed her lip. *I've been thinking about you all night.*

You really do like trouble.

I really do like you.

He didn't answer for a long time, and Jenny lay there, clutching her phone, wondering what she'd said that was wrong. She'd scared him off, hadn't she? But then finally her phone vibrated with a new incoming text.

I'm not a rich man, Princess. I get by. I do okay. But it wouldn't be enough for you.

Jenny read the text once, twice, and dropped her phone, shocked, and horrified.

What?

Eyes stinging, she blinked and made herself read the message again.

I get by. I do okay. But it wouldn't be enough for you.

She dropped the phone, feeling burned.

He thought she was a gold digger. He thought she was shallow. Superficial.

Oh God, he thought the worst of her.

He and Charles and who knew who else.

Maybe all of Marietta felt that way about her. Jenny Wright, gold digger.

Sickened, Jenny turned her phone off, putting it away for the night.

~

COLTON FELT LIKE a shit after sending that text but it needed to be said. After talking to Tricia earlier, and hearing Tricia say that Jenny was fragile and vulnerable right now, and might be looking for a rebound just to help her cope with losing Charles, Colton knew the best thing for them both was to step away.

It was important that he put distance between them now, before he really started to care. As it was, he cared a lot. Maybe too much.

Better to break things off now, cleanly, before either of them got entangled in something that wouldn't work.

Perhaps he shouldn't have made the comment about him

not having enough for her, but it was true. And he wasn't just talking about money, he was talking about his life, his emotions, his career.

Colton lived on the road. It was a hard life for a man but it could destroy a woman.

No, better to end it now so they both felt free. Besides, he wasn't looking for a wife, wasn't ready to settle down again. And if he ever did marry again, it'd be to a woman who wanted what he wanted—a modest home, kids, a good life based on simple pleasures. He earned decent money on the circuit. Four years ago he'd pulled in a quarter of a million dollars. Two years ago he'd made almost that again, but then handed over half of it to Lisa in the divorce, along with their big Tudor house that she'd had to have. It didn't take Lisa long to remarry, but Colton had learned his lesson. One couldn't buy happiness. One couldn't buy respect, either.

No, next time he fell in love, it'd be with a woman who'd love him for him, not what he had in the bank. She'd laugh at his jokes, and watch stupid shows with him, and then at night, she'd melt for him in bed. They'd cuddle close after sex and talk about their plans and dreams, like the babies they'd make and the places they'd go, and he'd be a rich man, not because of his investments, but because he'd fallen in love with a woman who was truly his best friend.

Chapter Ten

THERE WAS NO apology text from Colton in the morning.

There was no text at all.

Jenny didn't hear from him or see him for three days, and the first day she was just mad and hurt.

The second day she was hurt and still mad, but mostly hurt, as she didn't understand how something good had turned bad so fast.

And then on the third day she just didn't want to think about him anymore, or feel bad anymore. She'd had enough of feeling bad to last a lifetime so she focused on making plans for her future, which included returning to Chicago to figure out her next step. She wasn't sure if she would stay there and look for another job in the city, or if she'd return to Marietta, or move somewhere else. But she certainly couldn't figure out the future sitting in her parents' living room, so she booked a ticket on Amtrak, leaving from Malta, MT on Monday morning, getting into Chicago the next day.

She bought the cheapest ticket she could, which meant there would be no private sleeping car but it saved her a hundred dollars and her sister Mandy agreed to drive her to Malta, which was a good four-hour drive each way, but Mandy didn't work on Mondays at the hair salon and said she was happy to help.

After reserving the train ticket, Jenny and her sisters went to a five-thirty movie at the Palace Theatre and then headed to the Main Street Diner for pie and coffee, which was a long-standing Wright sister tradition.

It wasn't until they were seated at a wooden table in the middle of the diner that Jenny felt a strange current of energy sweep through her, a sizzling awareness that made her skin prickle and the hair on her nape rise.

She looked up, and there he was, just four tables away. He was with his mother having dinner. He wasn't looking at her. She wasn't even sure he'd seen her yet but Jenny didn't want to stay. She gathered her coat and purse and then saw her sisters looking at her, confused.

"What's wrong, Jen?" Charity asked.

"What's going on?" Mandy echoed.

Jenny shook her head, unable to explain. They didn't know about her dates with Colton and she didn't want them to know now, not after that last text message he'd sent her.

"I've just got a headache," she said, praying Colton didn't see them, praying she could avoid speaking with him.

Her mom had been right about him.

Her mom had warned her but Jenny hadn't listened.

"Food might help," Charity said.

Mandy nodded in agreement. "Maybe you need some soup. The chicken tortilla soup here is so good, and filling. Try that."

But Jenny didn't want pie or soup. She didn't think she could eat a bite.

She turned her head, glanced in Colton's direction and discovered he was looking at her.

Her stomach lurched. She flushed hot, then went cold. Jenny stumbled to her feet. "I'm going to get some air," she said. "I'll be right back, okay?"

Mandy frowned. "Should we order you something? The soup, maybe?"

Jenny nodded. She would have nodded at anything. She was too desperate to escape.

On the sidewalk outside of the diner, Jenny faced the turn-of-the-century domed courthouse in Crawford Park. Lights were trained on the gothic façade, making the courthouse appear bigger than it really was.

Jenny's hands balled into fists as she watched people cross the street, couples out walking arm in arm, and families with their strollers and baby carriages, all coming out to get a first glimpse of the decorations the city had put up for the big rodeo festivities this weekend.

There would be a parade Friday and a street dance, a pancake breakfast, and then the big steak dinner Saturday night before the rodeo finals on Sunday.

A half-dozen bands would be playing through the weekend, and the town was already filling up as cowboys and cowgirls arrived with their horse trailers, and settled in to be relaxed and rested for the competition this weekend.

The rodeo was a big deal in Marietta, and this year, the seventy-fifth, was the biggest deal yet, and folks were thrilled Colton Thorpe was the honorary chair.

Everyone loved Colton.

Everyone but her.

"You look mad as hell, darlin'," a deep voice drawled behind her.

Jenny stiffened at the sound of Colton's voice. "I am, so go away."

"You ought to come back inside. Your sisters want to be with you."

She shot him a scornful glance over her shoulder. "Why don't you go back inside, because your mother would like to be with you."

"Touché."

She shook her head, grinding her jaw tight. "I hate you."

His footsteps sounded behind her. He was walking towards her. "I deserve that."

"Yes, you do." She bundled her arms across her chest, trying to keep her crazy emotions in. She hated him. She did. But she also wanted still. Badly. "Now get lost before I punch you. Which you also deserve."

He laughed softly, amused. "Have you ever thrown a punch, princess?"

"No." He was standing right behind her now, so close she could feel his warmth and his intense male energy that prickled her skin and made her weak in the knees. "But it can't be that difficult," she said, glaring at him over her shoulder. "You make a fist and bam. In your face."

Colton's lips twitched, and creases fanned from his blue eyes as he choked back muffled laughter which just made her madder.

"I'm serious," she said.

"I know you are." But the corners of his mouth curved and his eyes gleamed and he was looking at her as if he wanted to do wicked things to her… deliciously wicked things…which of course were all the things she wanted him to do.

"I hate you," she added.

"You don't."

"I do."

He reached out to her, pulled her against him, and wrapped his arms around her, holding her close, warming her body with his. "No, you don't," he said, his deep voice dropping even lower to a husky growl. "You're just mad 'cause I hurt you. And I'm sorry for hurting you. It's the last thing I wanted to do."

"That's not true," she answered, her chest tightening, emotion making it hard to speak. "You meant to hurt me. You said the most awful words anyone could." Her breath hitched and her eyes burned and she bit down hard into her lower lip, determined not to cry. "I'm not a gold digger, Colton. I've never been a gold digger, and the fact that you'd say such a thing to me—"

He silenced the painful stream of words by covering her mouth with his. He molded her body to his, and persuasively kissed her, coaxing a reluctant response from her.

She'd been determined not to cave. She'd even put her hands up on his chest to push him away but his kiss was so good. He felt too good, and she leaned in to the kiss instead of pulling away.

By the time the kiss ended, it seemed as if half of Marietta had gathered to watch. Mandy and Charity were standing in the doorway watching, jaws dropped. Mrs. Thorpe was at the window. Even the waitresses had all paused to have a look.

"That was awfully public, Colton Thorpe," Jenny said, blushing and breaking free.

"People are going to talk," he agreed.

"Was that what you wanted?"

"No. You're what I want. But Tricia says you're fragile right now and I can't put pressure on you—"

"Screw Tricia." Jenny's shoulders squared and her chin lifted. "Yes, she's my friend, and your sister, but she doesn't know what she's talking about."

"You were supposed to get married Saturday."

"And it didn't happen. But that's because it wasn't supposed to happen." Her chin lifted higher, her eyes locking with his. “Maybe you were supposed to happen—” she held up a finger to keep him from interrupting, “—and I don’t mean as in marriage and mate and happily ever after, but in… this.” She gestured from him to her. “This… whatever it is… sex, lust, need. I don’t understand it but I don’t have to understand it. I don’t want to control it, either. I just want to feel it. To feel something. So, that’s what I think.” She swallowed hard, her courage receding. “Now you can say whatever it is you want to say.”

He looked at her a long moment then smiled, a slow sexy smile that promised serious heat. “I think it sounds good. I think it sounds great.”

He leaned towards her, kissed her on the lips. “So I’ll pick you up at nine.”

The corners of his mouth curled upward as he whispered mock-suggestively, “We’ll go somewhere dark and quiet and have a couple drinks and see if I can’t possibly satisfy your – uh – needs.”

HE PICKED HER up at nine and drove her to Livingston, to a little honky-tonk bar where a DJ was playing country songs, but no one in the bar cared that there wasn’t a live band. Everybody was on the dance floor, line dancing.

They drank a beer and then Colton, tugged her out with him onto the dance floor.

“I don’t know how,” she protested as they took their

places in the back row.

"You can't grow up in Marietta without knowing how to line dance."

"It's been ten years—"

"Just follow along. It'll come back to you." His blue eyes smiled down at her. "Just like riding a horse."

"I don't know how to ride a horse, either."

"I guess that's the next thing we need to do." And then the music started again and everyone was moving, right, left, forward, turning.

Jenny tripped over her feet as she struggled to remember the steps. She was mortified but Colton didn't seem to care, and he danced beautifully, all muscle in motion, graceful as anything, and it crossed Jenny's mind that he'd look beautiful on a horse, or a bucking bull.

He moved as if he'd been created for motion—taut, honed, strong.

They turned, she turned, and this time she didn't trip. She was beginning to get the steps. They were coming back.

She relaxed as they all stepped forward, then back, her hips looser, her steps firmer and more confident.

The music became rhythmic, hypnotic and it began to feel good, the body in motion, the warmth of moving, the energy of everyone dancing with her, around her.

She turned and Colton's gaze met hers, his gaze steady and warm, and for the first time she could remember, she actually felt beautiful.

Colton made her feel beautiful. Desirable.

They danced another couple of songs, before returning to their table. He was sitting next to her, his chair close to hers, and she could smell his fragrance and feel his warmth and it was hard to focus on anything but his long muscular legs, and the shape of his honed thighs, and how his big silver buckle rested just above the top of his zipper which made her stare at his crotch.

The fabric seemed to hug him all too well in that area, too.

She shouldn't look, but she couldn't help looking. She couldn't help thinking about the things she never thought about before, couldn't help being aware of how different she felt with Colton, how hungry she felt for more, and how she craved pleasure.

But it wasn't just physical pleasure she wanted.

She wanted Colton.

She loved Colton.

She always had.

Her eyes stung and her chest ached with the realization that Colton had always been the only man for her.

She'd agreed to marry Charles because she'd stopped believing in happy endings. She'd agreed to marry Charles because she'd stopped dreaming.

"What are you thinking about, darlin'?" Colton asked, carefully plucking the finest strand of hair tangling on her eyelashes and smoothing it away from her face.

She inhaled sharply at the brush of his thumb and finger against her face near her eye, and the way his knuckles skimmed her cheekbones, his skin warm, and instantly making her heart burn, and her body ache.

She loved him and it would hurt so bad when the weekend ended and they both left—he for the next rodeo and she back to Chicago—but it would hurt far worse not to have this moment with him now.

Because this moment was everything.

This was the moment she'd waited for her entire life.

"Come with me," Colton said abruptly, reaching for her hand and drawing her to her feet.

She followed him outside. She didn't ask why they were going out, or where they were going. Quite frankly at that moment she didn't care. As long as they were together she was good.

In the parking lot, Colton opened the door to his truck, and sat down on the edge of the bench seat, with his feet still planted on the asphalt parking lot and he pulled her close, settling a hand on her hip. "I owe you a proper apology, Jenny. I deliberately pushed you away because I thought it was the best thing, not just for me, but for you, too. But it was wrong, and hurtful, and I am so sorry I hurt you. You didn't deserve it. The truth is, you deserve so much better than me and I've had a hard time wrapping my head around the fact that you, princess, had this crush on me… and that you might actually still care for me."

"Why?" she asked, looking up into his eyes.

He shook his head, his hands on her hips, holding her close against him. "Because I'm a tough SOB. I'm not gentle and refined. Not a sophisticated city guy—"

"I never wanted that. Never, ever. I only ever wanted… tough SOB you."

He looked away, brow furrowing, eyes narrowing. He struggled for a moment to find the right words to speak. "But why?"

"I don't know. I've just always had a thing for you. Bad, tough SOB you." She reached up to clasp his face. She turned his head so she could look him in the eye. "I don't know why I like you so much. I don't know why I feel so good around you. But I do. Colton, I've gone through life ashamed. Ashamed of me, ashamed of our circumstances, aware that I'm one of those Wright girls that's all wrong." Her lips quivered as she struggled to smile. "But when I'm around you, I feel good. I feel… right." Tears filled her eyes. "So I don't care where this goes, or how it ends. I just want this, now, with you. I just want to be with you. And when it's over, I'll let you go and I won't say a word and I won't make you feel bad—"

"Jesus, Jen." Colton swore and dipped his head, his mouth covering hers. He kissed her fiercely, deeply, as he pressed a hand to the small of her spine, shaping her to him.

In her thin dress his touch felt like fire and ice and she couldn't move, frozen in place.

The kiss consumed her even as his hands explored her, his fingers sliding up her back, making her arch and shudder.

Against the hard cradle of his hips she could feel the cold silver buckle of his belt dig into her belly and the thick ridge of his erection on her inner thigh.

His hand stroked her again, up and down, and each time she arched, cat-like, her breasts pressing to his chest, her nipples tight and tender as she clenched inwardly, wanting more.

"You feel so good," he murmured, his mouth close to her ear, his breath making the skin beneath her ear tingle.

"You make me feel good," she answered breathlessly, as his hand slid up beneath her hair to cup her nape, fingers working her neck and then higher, into her scalp, and it was so delicious and erotic she nearly mewed with pleasure.

He lifted her hair up, and placed at kiss at her nape, one of his hands finding her breast, kneading the nipple as he kissed and nibbled from her nape to the side of her neck where she was so very sensitive. She gasped for air as he turned her mindless with pleasure, her body rippling with wave after wave of exquisite sensation.

He reached up under her short dress, stroked her inner thigh, and then higher to the edge of her lace panties.

"I want you," he said hoarsely, "but I can't take you here."

She rocked against his hand, sighing as he felt every sensitive spot of her through the lace. "Don't stop," she choked, voice trembling, legs trembling, body quivering from head to toe as Colton slid a finger beneath the lace and stroked her where she was warm and wet.

Charles never touched her like this. Charles had been very efficient about touch and sex. The less amount of energy he spent, the better.

Just like wanting her to drink her coffee black to keep her from wasting time on herself, he advocated sex without foreplay. That way he wasn't tired after and could get right back to work.

Colton didn't seem to mind touching. He was crooning compliments in her ear as he caressed her slick inner folds, teasing the delicate nub and then thrusting inside her.

"You're amazing," Colton whispered against his mouth, kissing her deeply as she felt the pressure build, the sensation so strong now they were nearly overwhelming.

He stroked her faster, thrusting deeper, managing to touch hit every pleasure point. She was going to come. She was going to shatter, here, like this, and she didn't care. She didn't care about anything but him and her and being together.

Colton drank in her cry of release with his kiss, as he brought her to orgasm. It had been so long since Jenny had climaxed she couldn't quite believe it'd happened.

Afterwards, he hauled her into the truck, on his lap, and held her, big arms wrapping around her, her cheek nestled to his chest.

Her heart was still pounding and her body was still warm and she closed her eyes and listened to his heartbeat. Such a strong, steady heartbeat.

She'd never forget tonight, she thought, breathing him in, never, ever.

"Jenny?"

Colton's deep voice made her lift her head. "Yes?" she whispered, looking up at him, seeing how the moonlight illuminated his profile, highlighting his high, hard chiseled cheekbone and strong, beautiful jaw.

"I want to be with you," he said. "I want to make love to you. But this is your night. This is about you. I can take you home. I can take you back in for some more beer and dancing. Or I can take you to the hotel room I've reserved here in Livingston and take these damn clothes off and make you mine. But it's up to you. I want you happy. I want to make you happy. So tell me, darlin'. What would you like to do?"

She searched his eyes, heart thumping. "I want to go to the hotel with you."

Chapter Eleven

HE'D CHECKED INTO the room earlier, so there was no wait or awkwardness at the front desk. They just went through the front door and up two flights of stairs to the room at the end of the hall.

Inside the room, Colton took charge, peeling Jenny's dress off and then pulling off her boots, and unhooking her lace bra before carrying her to the bed.

"You're still dressed," she said as he settled next to her.

He smiled crookedly. "My clothes are not the problem. I can get out of them quick."

She smiled back at him until he leaned over the corner of her mouth, and then her mouth, and then parted her lips with his so his tongue could flick the inside of her upper lip and suck on the tip of her tongue and make her melt.

She was melting. Once again.

She was aching. All over again.

He'd just brought her to climax in the parking lot and yet he was stirring her up again, making her blood pound and her heart race. He shifted over her, settling between her thighs, and she could feel the rub of his erection through the soft denim, could feel his hunger, and it was exciting. This heat between them was exciting. She welcomed it, wanting the fire, wanting to explore and be explored.

"Take your clothes off," she pleaded. "I want you, all of you. I'm desperate to feel your skin."

She helped him get the Western dress shirt unsnapped and off. She watched wide-eyed as he stepped from his Wranglers and then out of his briefs.

His erection sprang up, once freed, and she was amazed, as well as impressed.

Naked, Colton was back on the bed with her, drawing her into his arms, his hands stroking down her bare back to cup her butt.

She loved the feel of his warm chest against hers, and stroked the thick bronzed muscle of his pecs, and then higher to the honed plane that wrapped his shoulders and collarbone. "You have a seriously hot body," she whispered, awed.

He flipped her over onto her back, his head dipping to suckle her breast. Her hips lifted, arching against him as the warm wet tugs on her nipple made everything inside her tighten and ache.

He reached between them with one hand, found her, where she was soft and wet. He touched her, caressing her, making her hotter, wetter, more desperate.

It was a relief when he entered her, his big shaft sliding deep, filling her, sending streaks of sharp hot pleasure through every nerve.

He made love to her as if she were the most beautiful thing in the world, thrusting and stroking and kissing and stirring her senses until there was him and only him, and he didn't stop until she shattered with pleasure.

He pulled out just before he came, shuddering and releasing into the sheet to keep from coming on her.

"I'm on the pill," she said, kissing the side of his face, and then his mouth.

He rolled over onto his back, drew her to his side. "I didn't know," he said, his deep voice husky. "Should have asked. Should have certainly worn a condom. I bought some. You are hell on some self-control."

Jenny sighed, and curled closer, liking how her body fit his, feeling so comfortable with him. "Thank you. That was amazing."

"Was it now?" he asked, voice tinged with amusement.

"Mmmhmm. Better actually than I hoped."

He laughed and held her close and she fell asleep, still tucked safely at his side.

JENNY WOKE UP surprised for a moment to be in a strange bed with a strange body next to hers, and then she remembered where she was, and what had happened.

Colton had happened.

Her lips curved in a faint smile of appreciation.

Oh boy, had Colton happened.

She stretched a little and turning her face towards Colton, she discovered he was awake and watching her. "Hey," he said.

She smile shyly. "Hey, yourself."

"How are you feeling?" he asked.

"Amazing," she answered, unable to hide her grin. "How about you?"

"Pretty damn good."

She leaned over to kiss him. "Good."

He grabbed some pillows and propped his head up. "So, what's your plan, princess? What happens next?"

She rolled over onto her stomach and propped her chin in her hands, not yet ready for this. "Do we have to talk serious? It's kind of depressing after all that incredible lovemaking."

He reached out, stroked her hair, and then caressed her cheek. "We're not done, darlin. Just taking a break, letting you rest before I ride you hard and put you away wet."

Jenny giggled, just as he'd intended. "That sounds horrible and wonderful at the same time."

"That's because I am horrible and wonderful." His smile slipped. "When do you return to Chicago?"

She drew a deep breath. "Monday. Mandy's driving me to Malta to catch the Amtrak to Chicago."

"That's a five-hour drive."

"Four and a quarter the way Mandy drives."

He frowned. "That's a long way for her to go."

"The things we sisters do for each other."

"I'll take you," he said firmly. "I was heading out Monday anyway."

"I'm sure it's out of your way."

"But it'd give me four and a half hours more with you."

Jenny reached out to take his hand. She pressed a kiss to his palm. "That's nice of you."

"Better yet," he said, "why don't I drive you to Chicago and then I can fly from Chicago to San Francisco for next weekend's show at the Cow Palace."

"You're going to San Francisco next weekend?"

He nodded. "Need to get back riding, competing. The year's almost over. Every point counts at this stage of the game."

"How are you in the standings?"

"In third. But not too far back."

"That's good."

His head tipped and he studied her hard. "Why don't you come with me to San Francisco?"

"Don't tempt me. I've always wanted to go to California."

"Charles never took you there?"

"We went other places, when he had meetings and conferences." She ticked off the cities. "New York. Detroit. Boston. Atlanta." She thought hard. "And Phoenix."

"So you've seen a bit of the country."

She nodded. But California was top of her wish list.

She'd always wanted to see the Pacific Ocean and have chowder in one of those sourdough bread bowls she'd seen on the Travel Channel. You did that at Fisherman's Wharf, in San Francisco and you could see the Golden Gate bridge from there, too, she thought. She wanted to see the famous bridge, and ride a cable car, and if there was time, drive to the coast and visit Carmel and Monterey. She was pretty sure Clint Eastwood used to be mayor of one of them, although she couldn't remember which.

"Why can't you come with me?" he asked, tugging her up to him. He pulled her onto his chest. "What's keeping you here?"

Nothing. Nothing was keeping her here. She had friends and family here, but they didn't keep her here. They'd always be here. She could go and return…she could always go and return. Her family and friends would always welcome her back, welcome her home.

So that wasn't the issue.

"Is there a reason you need to be in Chicago?" he persisted.

Jenny shook her head. There was nothing for her in Chicago. Not anymore. Everything she wanted was right here. "No."

"Then what?" he asked, pushing a wave of her hair back from her face.

"I…" Her mouth opened, closed. She could think of reasons why she shouldn't go. Could think of people like Carol

Bingley and what they'd say. But people like Carol Bingley would talk no matter what she did. Or didn't do.

She couldn't control others. She couldn't change the past. She couldn't worry about a future that wasn't even here yet.

But she could live, and could have an adventure, a very romantic, impractical adventure with the only man she'd ever loved.

The man she hopelessly, madly, passionately loved.

"Yes," she said, eyes shining, pulse quickening.

"Yes?"

He clasped her face and kissed her deeply. "Damn, girl, but I am crazy about you."

She laughed.

"I'm serious," he said. "I'm falling… pretty damn hard and fast. If we're not careful, we might be getting hitched in Vegas on our way out West."

"Is that a promise or a threat?" she teased.

He drew her thighs apart so she sat up and straddled his naked hips. He was hard for her. "Maybe both, darlin'. What do you think of that?"

She sucked in a breath as he eased her down to him. "Whoa."

He arched a brow. "You haven't answered my question."

"I'm getting to it." She grinned mischievously as she rocked on him, making him groan. "I think it's going to be one hell of a ride. Take me with you, cowboy?"

EPILOGUE

Ten days later...

APPARENTLY SUMMERS IN San Francisco could be cold and foggy, but this October afternoon was stunning, with a blue sky so pristine there wasn't a cloud in sight. The Golden Gate bridge wasn't orange but red, almost like Colton's father's truck and Jenny loved the dramatic swooping red arc of the bridge against the green foothills and the dark blue water below an azure sky.

So many beautiful colors, so many new and exciting things to see.

This week she'd ridden in one of the city's famous cable cars, driven down crooked Lombard Street, eaten dim sum in historic China Town, had an incredible carne asada burrito south of Market, and bought a gorgeous glass snow globe of the San Francisco skyline at Union Square.

She'd also spent eleven hours in the emergency room of UCSF Medical Center, San Francisco's top-rated hospital, as they stitched up Colton's thigh and hip and set a cast around a leg full of broken bones.

The bull had got him this time.

One moment everything had been fine, and then the next, it was terrifying mayhem. Colton had made it to the Sunday finals and was one second shy of having a legitimate ride when the massive white spotted bull tossed Colton from his back, and then put his head down, and went after him, determined to finish him off.

They'd taken Colton to the hospital in an ambulance and they'd put Jenny in a cab to follow him.

When they finally allowed Jenny to join Colton, he took her hand and held it, and kissed her, before teasing her, saying, thank God it was just a little goring, and not life and death.

But the little goring meant that Colton might need some surgery later, when he returned to Tulsa. Colton was nonchalant about the prospect of surgery. It was part of his job—one of the hazards—and he was content to just wait and see how he mended, though he knew that the season was over for him. There would be no more competing until the new season began in Spring.

Jenny couldn't even think about Spring, or his next ride. It felt as if her heart had stopped when the bull went for Colton in the Cow Palace Arena.

When the bull put his head down, jamming his horn into Colton's thigh, she would have swapped places with him if she could. She loved him that much.

It might not make sense to anyone else, but Jenny had loved Colton her entire life. He was her person, her other half, and she couldn't image a future without him.

After Colton was discharged from the hospital Monday morning, they returned by cab to their hotel, where Colton slept for much of the day. He somehow he pulled himself together and insisted they head out mid-afternoon as he had somewhere special he wanted to take her for dinner.

They'd taken a cab from the hotel to Fisherman's Wharf to have that clam chowder in a sourdough bowl that Jenny had talked about.

So now they stood on the wharf, Colton leaning heavily on crutches, eating their soup which was good, but not that fantastic, gazing out at the majestic red-orange Golden Gate bridge, which was absolutely fantastic, watching the ferries come and go, while seagulls squawked and cried overhead.

Jenny had never been happier. Colton was safe. Colton adored her. Things were good—very, very good.

If Charles hadn't jilted her…

If Charles hadn't figured out that she was just poor Jenny Wright from Chance Avenue on the north side of Marietta…

"You all right?" Colton asked, gazing down at her, his jaw covered with the golden brown stubble of a beard. His eyes were still a little bloodshot. He had a bruise and a fresh gash on his right cheek. He'd had a hell of a night in the ring and then at the hospital, and yet here he was, playing tourist with her, for her.

What a good man. What a loving man.

Jenny felt so lucky. Lucky in love. Lucky in life.

She nodded and smiled up at him. "I'm great." She searched his face for signs of pain or exhaustion. He was incredibly tough, but she wanted to make sure he didn't push himself too hard. "How about you?"

"I'm awesome," he answered, adjusting the crutch, and moving his arm to slide around her. His head dropped for a quick kiss. "Because I have you."

She reached up to lightly touch his face, mindful of the cut and bruise. "I owe Charles a little thank-you for bringing me home to you."

"Oh, I owe him a bigger thank-you." Colton's eyes glinted. "Not that I'll tell him that. I don't like the guy. Have absolutely no respect for him."

"Fair enough."

"But we do need to get your car and things from Chicago."

"Yes."

"Where should we take them? To my place in Tulsa, or, should we look for a place of our own in Montana?"

She took a quick, hopeful breath. "Move back to Marietta?"

"There's some nice ranch land available right now. We could go looking at property together if you'd like. I'm not going to be traveling for a while. Could be a good time to look for a place we can call home."

She searched his eyes, feeling dazzled and breathless. "Seriously?"

He nodded. "But I wouldn't want to get a place together unless I thought we were really going to be together." He fell silent, his forehead furrowing. "I want a future with you, Jenny. I want a family with you. Those babies you talked about, I want that, too."

"Yes," she whispered.

"I know it's awfully soon to be talking about getting married, but I love you. You're my girl. You're the one for me. I'd get down on my knee darlin', but I can't—"

"It's okay," she interrupted, tears filling her eyes. "Don't do that. The stitches and staples might come out and then we'd have to go back to the hospital and that would be awful."

He laughed, chucked his soup bowl in a trash can, and reached into his pocket, withdrawing a little velvet jewelry box. "But I do have a ring, and I want it on your finger. That is, if it's a yes…?"

"It's a yes, yes, yes." She tossed her soup bowl and mindful of Colton's crutches, pressed close to him, kissing him once before giving him her hand, so he could slide the brilliant white diamond solitaire onto her finger. "Oh, it's beautiful."

"You're beautiful," he answered, gently kissing her forehead, the tip of her nose, and then her lips. "And you're mine."

She smiled through her tears. "That's right. Always, and forever."

Jenny Wright from Chance Avenue was the luckiest, happiest girl in the world.

THE END

New York Times bestselling author Jane Porter's contemporary romance series….

The Taming of the Sheenans

The Sheenans are six powerful wealthy brothers from Marietta, Montana. They are big, tough, rugged men, and as different as the Montana landscape.

Christmas at Copper Mountain
Book 1: Brock Sheenan's story

Tycoon's Kiss
Book 2: Troy Sheenan's story

The Kidnapped Christmas Bride
Book 3: Trey Sheenan's story

Taming of the Bachelor
Book 4: Dillion Sheenan's story

A Christmas Miracle for Daisy
Book 5: Cormac Sheenan's story

The Lost Sheenan's Bride
Book 6: Shane Sheenan's story

Available now at your favorite online retailer!

ABOUT THE AUTHOR

New York Times and USA Today bestselling author of forty-nine romances and women's fiction titles, **Jane Porter** has been a finalist for the prestigious RITA award five times and won in 2014 for Best Novella with her story, Take Me, Cowboy, from Tule Publishing. Today, Jane has over 12 million copies in print, including her wildly successful, Flirting With Forty, picked by Redbook as its Red Hot Summer Read, and reprinted six times in seven weeks before being made into a Lifetime movie starring Heather Locklear. A mother of three sons, Jane holds an MA in Writing from the University of San Francisco and makes her home in sunny San Clemente, CA with her surfer husband and two dogs.

Thank you for reading

Take Me, Cowboy

If you enjoyed this book, you can find more from all our great authors at TulePublishing.com, or from your favorite online retailer.

TULE

PUBLISHING

Made in the USA
Middletown, DE
17 September 2020

20062733R00097